HANDSOME DEVIL

DELANEY DIAMOND

Garden Avenue Press

Dante Escarra lined up the golf club against the ball and then took a swing. There was a low pop and the ball shot into the net at the end of his office, which kept it from crashing through one of the many windows that gave him a spectacular view of the Houston skyline.

A couple of years ago, he turned one end of his huge office into a miniature driving range, allowing him to practice during breaks throughout the workday. The exercise also helped him think. He'd solved many problems with a golf club in hand.

As he set another ball atop the tee, the muffled sound of raised voices came to him from the other side of his office's double doors. Cocking his head, he listened closely and was about to walk into the outer office to find out what was going on when one of the doors thrust open from the other side.

He watched in shock as the last person he expected to see flounced into the room on a pair of black stiletto heels and a determined expression on her face.

Annabelle Buchanan. His ex-wife.

All the hairs on the back of his neck stood at a 90-degree angle.

"I'm sorry, Dante," his male office manager said, glaring at the back of Annabelle's head. "I turned my back for a second, and she slipped past me."

Most people couldn't get past Sebastian because he intimidated them at over six feet with the build of an athlete. Not Annabelle, though. No one intimidated her. She was as vicious as she was beautiful.

"That's okay, Sebastian. I'll take over from here."

Sebastian sent one more angry glance at his ex-wife and walked out.

Annabelle shot a fake smile at Dante. "Hello, darling."

Her tone was soft, like the low purr of a lioness angling to pounce on unsuspecting prey. The combination of the endearment and the sound of her voice made a tingle of awareness skitter over his skin.

Her cultured voice had a soothing lilt. He used to keep her on the phone just to hear her speak. Other times, he laid his head in her lap and told her about his dreams while she listened and then gave her opinion in the same voice, helping him work through various scenarios. She had been the respite he needed in an otherwise challenging and chaotic world. A long time ago.

Carefully, Dante placed his golf club against the wall. "Get out." He wasn't going to waste time being polite or exchanging pleasantries.

"Don't be so nasty. Is that any way to talk to your ex-wife?" She batted her eyelashes at him.

"It's the only way to talk to an ex-wife who's a soul-sucking demon."

Her laughter was throaty and sexy, and the way his dick jumped at the sound pissed him off.

"You haven't changed a bit, Dante. You're as charming as ever. Do you think you could put aside the animosity for five minutes and listen to what I have to say? I came to talk to you about something important."

She crossed the room, bringing the scent of orange blossoms and sweet jasmine with her, and plopped her taupe Bottega

Veneta tote on the edge of his huge L-shaped desk made of glass. His eyes followed the movement of her body—a body that, at one time, he'd had the right to explore and had done so with enthusiasm at every opportunity.

As usual, she was incredibly well put together. Today, she wore a blue and orange print sheath dress that completely covered her with a high neckline and long sleeves, but the outfit clung to her mouth-watering curves in a sinfully provocative way. The dress might as well have been painted on, emphasizing her full breasts and great ass. Her dark hair contained honey-blonde highlights and tumbled onto her shoulders with the faux carelessness only a professional stylist could manufacture.

Her makeup was immaculate, highlighting her long lashes and brightening her golden-brown skin—the result of having a white father and Black mother. Her skin glowed with health and vitality—no doubt from the magic of the best regularly scheduled facials money could buy.

Against her swarthy features, her eyes were a striking gray with hints of blue. Bronze lipstick brought attention to full lips that dominated her face and reminded him of the power they'd held over him when he had been foolish enough to fall for her charms.

"I'm not interested in anything you have to say, so don't waste your time."

"Time with you is never a waste," Annabelle said sweetly, posing with one hand on her hip.

Dante chuckled to himself in an effort to cool the heat rising in his body. "What game are you playing, Anna? You and I have not spent any time together since we divorced."

"Not true. We see each other now and again, and I saw you as recently as six months ago at the Fight Hunger in Houston event. Don't you remember?"

They had seen each other from time to time over the years, at various social and industry events around the city. Instead of dwindling, their animosity had grown with each brief encounter.

Instead of time healing their wounds, it caused them to linger and fester.

Annabelle continued. "You arrived with that woman who calls herself a model—oh, what was her name?" She lifted her gaze to the ceiling and snapped her fingers twice before locking eyes with him again. "Tatiana, right? Where did you find her?"

"If I didn't know better, I would say you're jealous. But you'd have to have feelings to be jealous, no?"

She laughed, completely unmoved by the insult. "You've always thought I was unfeeling, but nothing could be further from the truth. I feel deeply."

That was halfway true, at least. She cared deeply about her family and the people she was closest to. As her husband, however, he had not been able to elicit the same love and compassion she expressed toward others. He'd tried but been unable to make her happy, and one day, she simply cut him off at the knees when she became tired of the marriage.

He couldn't say he was surprised, but he'd nonetheless been blindsided when she left. He still carried major resentment over the way she skipped out of their marriage and ran back home to her father's mansion.

"You came here for a reason. What do you want?"

"You should take a seat for this," Annabelle said, waving toward his leather chair.

She spoke in a lowered voice. Her seduction voice—low and throaty and bringing back memories that lashed his skin with heat.

His eyes narrowed in distrust. "Why do I need to sit down?"

"I'm not sure you'll like what I'm about to say." She gave a careless, one-shoulder shrug.

"Tell me so we can get this meeting over with, and I can go back to more important tasks, like practicing my golf swing." He glanced at the Patel Philippe watch on his wrist. "You have sixty seconds to explain why you're here, and then I'm calling security to escort you out."

She let out an exaggerated sigh. "Fine. I have a proposition for you."

"I cannot wait to hear it," Dante said in a dry voice.

Another fake smile. "My father plans to step down as the CEO of Buchanan & Buchanan within the next few months."

"Time is ticking. You have twenty-seven seconds."

"Be patient, darling. I promise you'll want to hear this," she said, strolling over to the bar where he kept beverages for guests. She poured herself a glass of water and took a sip before turning to face him.

"Seventeen seconds."

Annabelle arched an eyebrow. "When he steps down, he plans to recommend a merger to the board—a merger with his friend's company, Strong Technology, Inc. They're a privately owned firm specializing in smart home technology to modernize residential properties and make them more efficient. Daddy has threatened to go through with this merger for years."

"What does that have to do with me?" Dante tapped his watch as a reminder.

"Nothing, directly." Annabelle finished the water and carefully placed the glass on a silver tray atop the bar. "Except for the proposition I mentioned. Instead of merging the companies and having Albert Strong take over as CEO, I want Daddy to recommend *me* as CEO to the board, but unfortunately, he won't because of his traditional values."

A brief flash of pain zipped across her eyes, so fast he almost missed the emotion.

"That's your problem. Again, what does your father's decision have to do with me?"

She looked him squarely in the eyes. The haughty indifference disappeared, and a tough negotiator took its place. "My father admires and respects you. He thinks you're a great businessman because of all you've accomplished in the ten years since our divorce. You've made quite a splash in the commercial real estate market. Therefore, my proposition is simple. I want to take over my father's company, and I need you to help me make that happen. I'm proposing that you and I remarry."

Dante cocked his head toward her in disbelief. "Excuse me, I misunderstood what you said. My English is not so good."

"Your English is excellent. Probably better than mine at this point, so I know you understood perfectly what I said. I'm suggesting we get married again—a marriage of convenience, if you will. A mutually beneficial arrangement for both parties, you and me. My father will be happy to have you back in the family because he did like you, and now he has newfound respect for you thanks to all your accomplishments. Based on a conversation we had, I'm convinced he would recommend me for the CEO position *if* he thought you'd be involved in helping me with B&B, as needed. Our marriage would be temporary. Sometime after I take the reins of the company, you and I will have an amicable divorce. Not right away, of course. We want our reunion to be believable, but we simply split because we couldn't make our marriage work for a second time."

Dante folded his arms over his chest. Unbelievable.

"Your plan is to remarry and trick your father into believing you and I are happily married, so he will hand over the company to you when he steps down? That's your plan?"

She smiled brilliantly. "Yes."

"Ah *querida, t'eres loca,*" Dante said.

Then he burst out laughing.

2

From the scowl on Annabelle's face, she didn't appreciate his laughter.

"What's so funny?" she demanded.

Dante stopped laughing and studied her with amusement. "You cannot be serious. Tell me that you're joking."

"I'm not."

"You want *me* and *you* to get married again?"

"Yes," she answered in a voice suggesting she didn't understand what the big deal was.

Dante ambled behind his desk and tapped his fingers on the top of the leather chair. "Okay, I'll play along. You said you want a temporary marriage. For how long?"

"No more than one year. Long enough to make the world believe we were serious and gave the relationship a good try. Our lives won't change much, except that we live together."

"You have a very mercenary point of view."

"Being mercenary has nothing to do with it. I don't want Albert Strong to steal what's rightfully mine," she said with a hard note in her voice.

"And you want to prove to Daddy Dearest that you can handle the work, despite being a mere woman."

Her cheeks turned a pinkish hue because his words hit a nerve.

"My relationship with my father is none of your concern," she said in a low voice. "What do you think of my proposal?"

"I already told you what I think."

"That was your first impression because you don't know what you get out of the deal."

"What *do* I get?"

"Access."

He couldn't help himself. His gaze skimmed her shapely hips and the fullness of her breasts, and he idly wondered if she'd come dressed like that to tempt him.

His dick lifted in his pants at the memory of the fiery love they used to make. Annabelle was as insatiable as he was, though at first she pretended to be shy and demure. They had been very young when they married, only twenty and twenty-one, both with very few sexual partners. Unfortunately, with the typical naïveté of a young married couple, they tried to solve every problem between the sheets because it had been the one area where they communicated best—right up until she left him.

"Not *that* kind of access," Annabelle said, her voice filled with the Arctic bite of the North Pole. "I meant you'll have access to Houston's inner circle and one man in particular. Nolson Hilderbrandt. A little birdie told me that he's quietly looking for a buyer for the Hilderbrandt Plaza, and if I remember correctly, you once mentioned you'd kill to get your hands on that building."

¿Qué? Dante's heart took off at a gallop, but he maintained a calm exterior.

No way Nolson would sell that building voluntarily. It had been in his family for decades.

The Hilderbrandt family owned the iconic Hilderbrandt Plaza, which dominated the Houston skyline and was the tallest building in the state. There had been whispers of solvency issues in the family business, and allegedly they had paid debts late in recent months. If Nolson was going to sell the Plaza, that could only mean one thing. They needed the money.

Word had not gotten to Dante yet that Nolson, the forty-something-year-old current head of the family business after his father passed several years ago, was planning to sell—but that was no surprise. Unlike his father, Nolson didn't spend much time in the spotlight, preferring to stay at his mansion with his much younger wife when he wasn't running the family empire. Also, there was the murky, complex class system dominating the upper echelons of Houston society.

Nolson came from old money, having inherited generational wealth which kept his family in social prominence. Dante was new money and had amassed his fortune within the past decade. The line of demarcation between the two worlds had never mattered to him before, but in this instance, the boundary kept him behind the curve, on the outside of the most important deal of his life.

Dante wanted the building so badly he could almost taste the glass and steel. Such a prominent property would be handled in a private sale between friends or business acquaintances. More than likely, the buyer would be someone in Nolson's immediate social network or referred by a person in their group.

Dante didn't adhere to the same social traditions and thus wasn't part of the circle the Hilderbrandts belonged to. He was a member of the country club, but he didn't get invited to the private dinners at the estates of the old money elites. He attended charity balls and philanthropic galas, but there were other, smaller events where his name never made the list. Clifton and Annabelle Buchanan, on the other hand, would be on the list. Like Nolson, Clifton's wealth was generational in nature.

A devilish grin touched Annabelle's lips. "If you still want the property, I can get you an audience with Nolson."

If Dante got an audience with him, he was convinced he

could make the man an offer he couldn't refuse, and he'd finally accomplish the one goal that had eluded him for years. Hilderbrandt Plaza would be the crown jewel in his portfolio of properties and raise his profile even higher.

Keeping his gaze neutral, he took in the knowing expression on Annabelle's face. She was like a shark and could smell blood the same as the marine predator.

"I'll think about it," he said.

Displeased with the answer, she straightened her spine, which made her breasts jut out in a tantalizing way.

"What's there to think about? Do you want the building or not?"

"I'm... interested."

"Then we'll both receive what we want if we work together. I'll receive my rightful inheritance, and you'll own the most iconic building in Texas."

"You're talking about getting married again. Did you forget what happened the first time?"

"Of course not. I have the scars as a reminder."

"So do I, or do you think you're the only one who suffered in our marriage?"

"You? Suffer? Please." She laughed airily.

Dante ground his teeth together, tempted to throttle her where she stood. She brought out the worst in him.

"Are you suggesting you were the only one who suffered?"

"I'm suggesting you can cut the bullshit and admit you want the Hilderbrandt building, and if we work together, we can both succeed. We didn't do a good job of working together when we were married, but I think we can do a better job the second time around, with such high stakes at risk."

"Have you considered all the ins and outs of your proposal? Would we be able to see other people, or do you expect me to live like a monk during the entire year that we're together?"

"The marriage will remain unconsummated, of course, which

means you'll have to be discreet with your extramarital liaisons. I wouldn't want anyone to find out and think you'd broken my heart."

"Come now, Anna. No one would believe something so ridiculous," Dante said. "You'd need to have a heart to break. There's nothing but an empty hole in your chest."

Her gray-blue eyes flashed in annoyance, which secretly made him happy.

"When do you think you can give me an answer?" she asked.

"I can give you an answer right now. The answer is no."

"That's not the final answer, and you know it. You'll think about the offer because, though you don't like me very much, the opportunity to own the Hilderbrandt property is too juicy to resist. I'll give you three days, and then I'll go down the list and pick someone else."

"There are others?"

"Of course, darling. I was giving you first dibs because I had something to offer that I suspected you couldn't resist."

"Or there's no one else, and you're hiding your desperation," Dante drawled.

"I'm never desperate." Annabelle picked up her purse from the chair. "I came to you first because we have history, and I'm a nice person. I want to see you succeed."

"You made your offer out of the goodness of your heart?" Dante asked sarcastically.

"Of course. You know how generous I can be," she said without a flicker of irony.

She pouted prettily, and his dick jumped. Memories of the countless times she was on her knees before him came flooding back with the force of a burst dam.

If he could, he would drag her to her knees now. Would she purr and moan without breaking eye contact like she used to? She used to love giving blow jobs and would get turned on while his eyes rolled back in head.

"Impossible, since as I pointed out before, you need to have a heart. Which you don't."

"You don't know me at all, Dante. You never did."

Something they could agree on, but the heaviness of the words made him narrow his eyes, and she turned away before he could properly assess her thoughts.

Annabelle slipped the purse onto the crook of her arm. "We'll chat soon. Remember, you have seventy-two hours. Then I'm moving on. Tah-tah." She waved and then waltzed out the door with her fine ass swaying and her head held high.

Before the door swung closed behind her, Sebastian pushed it open, as if he'd been waiting just outside. He closed the door and looked at Dante.

"What was that about?"

Dante sat down and rubbed his jaw. "Annabelle came by to make me an offer."

"What could she possibly have to offer?"

Sebastian was more than his employee. They had been friends for years.

"She wants to get married again, so I can help her get her father's company, and in exchange, she gets me an audience with Nolson Hilderbrandt."

Sebastian's eyes widened. "Did you say *marry* her?"

"That's right." Dante quickly outlined Annabelle's idea.

"You're not seriously considering this plan, are you? There must be another way to land the Hilderbrandt building."

Sebastian knew about his strong desire to own the landmark.

Dante leaned forward. "They're having money problems, which means Nolson might be close to selling, and I can't let the plaza slip through my fingers."

Sebastian raked his fingers through his blond hair. "But marriage, to *her*? What did you tell her you would do?"

Dante propped his feet atop the desk, his leather chair squeaking as he leaned back. "I told her no."

"Did you mean it?"

Dante's gaze met his friend's. "I haven't decided yet, but this potential opportunity with Anna reminds me of something my mother used to say, and the lesson she tried to teach me."

"What did she used to say?" Sebastian asked.

Dante smiled. "A patient man will always eat ripe fruit."

3

A   nnabelle walked to the elevator and kept her eyes
     straight ahead while bitter thoughts swirled in her head.
     She hated that she had to come to Dante for help,
but bottom-line, she needed him and was counting on him
needing her. If he accepted her offer, perhaps they could refrain
from killing each other long enough to actually help each other.

She had hoped for a positive answer to her proposal today
but in reality had known such optimistic expectations were
wishful thinking. Dante probably hated her more than she
disliked him. After all, she had been the one to walk away from
their marriage without so much as a note of warning.

Yes, he definitely hated her.

All the way down in the elevator, she held tight to her self-
control, cognizant of the camera in the back left corner of the
cabin. She didn't want word getting back to Dante that she had
fallen apart after leaving his office.

By the time she exited the building and marched through the
covered parking lot to her car, she was barely holding on by a
thread. Quickly, she opened the car door and settled into the
leather seat of her Mercedes coupe. Safely ensconced in the interior, she released a tremulous breath.

There was a lot at stake. She could not let that liar, Albert Strong, take control of the company. Her father thought he was making the right decision by having the two companies merge, but Albert had let slip to her that when the companies did merge, he planned to lay off a large percentage of the long-term employees and hire new ones at reduced salaries. She couldn't let him destroy those employees' lives. When she told her father, the bastard denied his plans and said she must have misunderstood. And her father believed *him* over her.

She knew a lot of the staff. Not only from working there, but from when she was a kid coming by her father's company over the years.

Like Lawrence, who worked his way up from a property manager to managing his own portfolio of properties. She used to always stop by his office and pluck candy from the jar on his desk. What would his wife and kids do if he was forced out of the company where he'd worked for more than two decades?

Then there was Julie, a ten-year employee whose contacts at the zoning office got their permits quickly pushed through during time-critical moments in their property development phases. Her elderly parents had a number of age-associated ailments and depended on her for financial support. How would all their lives be impacted if Julie was forced to leave and take a lower-paying job?

"Over my dead body," Annabelle muttered to herself.

Marriage to Dante was the only way she envisioned holding on to the company. Her father didn't believe she was capable of taking the helm, which left a sour taste in her mouth, but she couldn't completely blame him for his thoughts.

As a younger woman, she hadn't been particularly interested in Buchanan & Buchanan Properties and had spent most of her time shopping and taking lavish vacations. She cringed when she remembered how carefree and lacking of responsibility her life had been. She had been spoiled for sure.

On the other hand, her half brother, Clifton Jr. from her

father's first marriage, had been reared to take over the company. Eight years older than Annabelle, he had been a daredevil, participating in extreme sports whenever he wasn't working side by side with their father. Unfortunately, he participated in one daring escapade too many. When she was twelve years old, he died tragically in a mountain climbing accident at the young age of twenty.

His death devastated their family and shined a spotlight on Clifton Senior's old school beliefs. His only son, his heir, was gone—along with the tradition of passing the reins of the family business to a male member of the family. He had no problem paying for his daughter's education, but he didn't believe a woman's place was heading up the company.

Clifton was set in his ways, and Annabelle had long ago given up trying to change his opinion. His prejudice hurt, but she loved him nonetheless and knew without a doubt that he loved her. He was a wonderful father in other ways—supportive and willing to satisfy every one of her needs and wants.

However, he had always admired Dante's drive. "He's going to be something one day," her father had said, with the certainty that came with age. Over the years, he'd watched his prediction come true and been impressed with how Dante built a privately owned commercial real estate empire worth over two billion dollars.

Several weeks ago, out of desperation, she had hinted at a reunion with Dante, and her father had been surprised but expressed his enthusiasm for the idea. Now she had to deliver. A sexless marriage to Dante, where they both obtained what they wanted and then went their separate ways could work. If she married him again, her father would become comfortable allowing her to take over because Dante, though he wouldn't work for the company, would be right by her side, and she could consult with him.

She just needed her ex to say yes.

There was no one else she could count on, on such short

notice, though she pretended she had other options. She expected her father to retire within the next few months, therefore time was of the essence. All she had to do was marry Dante and stay married to him for a year, for appearance's sake. A small price to pay to protect the jobs of the people she considered family and keep Buchanan & Buchanan in the family.

Annabelle dialed her best friend's number and lifted the phone to her ear. Lacey Locke was the only person she'd told about her plans, and she was sworn to secrecy.

"Did you see Dante and make the offer?" Lacey asked, in lieu of saying *hello*.

"I did," Annabelle confirmed.

"What did he say?" She sounded breathless with anticipation.

"First, he said he'd think about the offer, and then he said no. I'd hoped for a different answer, but it's what I expected. *But* he's definitely interested in the Hilderbrandt building. I could tell." Her eyes followed a man rushing from his vehicle toward the parking garage's elevator.

"Do you think it'll be enough?"

Annabelle gently gnawed her thumbnail. "It has to be. I have to move quickly before Daddy recommends the merger to the board, which will probably happen at the next meeting. I remember the way Dante talked about that building, and I'm certain he still wants it."

"For your sake, I hope you're right. How did you feel, spending time with your ex-husband alone?"

Heat flamed her cheeks. Her entire body had heated in Dante's presence, but she believed she'd played it off well.

"I've seen him around town before."

"You know what I mean," Lacey said.

Annabelle bit the corner of her lip and prepared a diplomatic answer because she did know what her friend meant. Those times she and Dante had encountered each other at events around the city, they carefully kept their distance from each other. They rarely spoke, but their paths didn't cross as often as one would think. They moved in different sectors of the real estate world, where he dominated commercial real estate, and her father held a smaller but nonetheless influential role in residential real estate.

The last time she saw him—at the Fight Hunger in Houston event—the way he had sipped champagne in a black tux and kept his dark eyes locked on her as she spoke had made her self-conscious and very aware of his commanding presence. His dark-brown eyes appeared hard as steel when he looked at her. That night she'd walked away as soon as possible, but by then, her nerves were shit, and her limbs were shaking.

Dante had this innate ability to shrink every room he entered and compel the eyes of women and men to follow him as he moved. He was more devastatingly handsome than when they first met, and in the past ten years, his face had matured, and his body had bulked up as if he spent more time in the gym than he used to.

She never forgot the first time she laid eyes on him. He and his friend Sebastian crashed a private party at Lola, one of the most exclusive restaurants in town, "to see how the other half lived and make connections" she learned later. He intrigued her right away with his rugged good looks and spine-tingling accented English. He was much more polished now but couldn't hide the roughness that remained around the edges.

His lips were still temptingly curved, and her name on his tongue continued to have the same effect as years before. He always called her Anna, and the way he said her name, breathing it in his deep voice, made her toes curl in her Loro Piana heels. He had worked hard to lose his accent, and it was almost gone now. But he didn't sound like a typical Texan, and the way he pronounced certain words sent a delicious shiver down her spine.

"We traded insults, and at the end of the day, all I can do is wait. I gave him a few days to get back to me."

"He has the entire weekend?" Lacey said.

"Yes."

"And if you don't hear from him by Monday?"

Annabelle briefly closed her eyes. "I'd rather not think negatively right now. I'm going to stay optimistic and believe that by Monday afternoon he'll give me a call and agree to the marriage. Then we can work out the details with our lawyers."

"I hope you know what you're doing," Lacey said.

"Don't I always?" Annabelle asked, with more confidence than she felt.

"Keep me posted?"

"Of course."

"Okay, I have to return to work. I received a request for a custom-designed dress, and I need to tweak the sketch based on feedback from the client. Talk to you soon."

After she hung up, Annabelle contemplated what she would do if Dante reached out. She already had an attorney on standby to prepare the contract for the one-year term, as well as ready to prepare a prenup, so Dante didn't have any rights to her father's company after the divorce. She had to be careful with him. Around Houston, people had resorted to calling him *el diablo guapo*—the handsome devil. They spoke about him with awe and admiration sprinkled with copious amounts of fear.

And they didn't call him the devil for nothing. He was known to circle businesses like a hyena, waiting for the right moment to swoop in and take control. As part of his reign, he gobbled up smaller companies that competed against him and capitalized on services they provided better than Escarra Commercial Real Estate did.

Dante had moved to the United States from Venezuela and started from the bottom, purchasing his first property in a booming part of town, which allowed him to eventually grow his company to the business it was today. He was smart as hell and had accumulated his wealth at a startling rate and, at times, with questionable actions, therefore he could very well try to take Buchanan & Buchanan from her.

She hoped Hilderbrandt Plaza was enough of an enticement to convince him to agree to her proposal. If not, she had no more ideas, which meant the merger would go through because her father's recommendations carried a lot of weight with the board.

She sighed and started the car.

Dante *had* to say yes.

❧ 4 ❧

"**Y**ou're not coming in?" Stella asked.

"No," Dante replied with a shake of his head.

Stella was one of the most beautiful women in Houston. Tall and dark-haired, she had crystal-blue eyes and a winning smile. As a real estate agent, she racked up millions in commissions every year, always landing in the top three of agents in the state.

She was one of the few people he could talk business with for hours, and tonight, he'd taken her to Chateau Bianchi, an upscale French restaurant in the heart of Houston. Regular customers had to wait months for a chance to eat there, but Dante was no regular customer, and he took full advantage of the fact.

Establishments like Chateau Bianchi always kept off-the-book tables available for people like him, and when his assistant called to make a reservation for the night, the restaurant accommodated him. He was amazed things like that happened. He, an immigrant from Caracas, Venezuela, who had arrived in this country with a dream and very little money, was able to get a table at the finest establishments—no matter what. Simply because of the zeroes in his bank account.

They sat at a well-appointed table in the dining room and ate a delicious dinner. He had fully intended to spend the night with Stella's legs wrapped around his waist, yet the last thing he wanted to do was enter her condo.

"It has been a long week. I'm going home now so I can wake up early in the morning and get some work done."

"Tomorrow is Sunday. You work too much," she moaned with pouting red lips, trailing a finger down the front of his shirt.

He smiled. "I like to play, too."

"When will you play with me?" Stella eased into his personal space, gazing up at him with her lips parted in a sensual invitation to kiss.

Dante had run through his share of women over the years—in state, out of state, in other countries—and under normal circumstances, the move would have him rock hard and ready to go. He didn't have the urge for sex tonight, though. Not after seeing his beautiful but conniving ex-wife yesterday. The entire time he'd been on this date, all he could think about was golden-brown skin and cool gray-blue eyes framed by long lashes.

"As soon as I have some time. I promise." He took Stella's hand and pressed a kiss to the knuckles.

"What's going on with you tonight? You seemed rather quiet over dinner."

"Was I?"

"Yes, you were. Last time you were more talkative."

"Not too much, I hope."

"More than tonight," she said pointedly. "Is something wrong?" She tilted her head to the right, brow furrowing with concern.

He couldn't tell her what had happened yesterday. Annabelle must be very desperate to come to him with such an outlandish idea, outright refusing to accept his answer of *No*.

"I have a lot on my mind," Dante admitted.

"Obviously. Anything you want to talk about?"

"Nothing that would interest you," he replied, softening the dismissal with a smile.

She pouted prettily. "All right. I'll leave you alone, but remember, I won't wait forever."

With that last warning, Stella let herself into the condo. She paused and cast another baleful look at him, perhaps hoping he would change his mind. Her shoulders dropped slightly when she realized he wouldn't.

"Good night," she whispered. Then she quietly shut the door.

Dante strolled down the hall to the elevator, nodding briefly at the couple who exited before walking into the cabin. On the ride down, his thoughts once again turned to Annabelle.

Had she given him the full story?

Outside, he approached the valet stand. He usually drove himself everywhere and didn't have a full-time driver, preferring to contract with a service as the need arose.

"Hello," he said, holding out his card.

The young woman took it, a smile of interest spreading across her face. "*Hello*. I'll be right back." She raced off.

As he waited, he thought about how much his life had changed. People believed he was a ruthless, cutthroat businessman—and in many ways, he was and welcomed the characterization. He knew what it was like to go without and never wanted to be in such a position again.

Years ago, his father had been injured on the job, which cut the family income in half. Then the Venezuelan economy collapsed, and they were hit with hyperinflation and high unemployment. As the eldest son, he moved to the States at the age of seventeen to start a new life and do what he could to help his family. He worked multiple jobs to make ends meet and hid his struggle from them by prioritizing necessary purchases instead of wants, so he could send money home. Having crossed the threshold into billionaire status, he had one goal—to acquire more. All because he learned a valuable but brutal lesson early on.

He had been working multiple jobs for a couple of years, one of which was shining businessmen's shoes early in the morning. He hated the work, but the tips were great if he did a good job. There was one man he had seen a few times and admired.

The guy dressed sharply in obviously expensive suits, pulled his cash from a gold money clip, and had an air of success about him. One day, he sat in Dante's chair, and Dante worked up the nerve to ask advice on how to become successful like he was. He would never forget the man's reaction.

He laughed.

Laughed in Dante's face.

"Where did you go to college? What skills do you have other than shining shoes?" He leaned forward, gaze meeting Dante's. "Do yourself a favor and be realistic, kid. People will tell you that you can be anything you want to be, but it's not true. The people who start where you are and succeed are the exceptions, not the rule. You need knowledge. Education, preferably Ivy League. You have to dress the part. You, my friend, have none of that. I can barely understand what you're saying with that thick accent. Maybe one day you'll find a job working in a nice place—I don't know. But successful like me? That'll never happen."

He chuckled to himself, as if the thought of Dante's success was preposterous.

The burn of humiliation seared Dante's cheeks. He had been looking for something, reaching out a hand for help from someone he admired, but he'd had the same hand smacked in the most unkind way.

That executive wasn't the first person to express the belief that Dante wouldn't amount to much. He'd grown accustomed to people dismissing him because of his clothes and accent, but those words had been openly condescending and extra cruel. They cut deeper than any slight he had experienced since he migrated to the country.

Stepping down from the chair, the man pulled a twenty from his gold money clip and tossed the bill on the bottom step. "You need it more than I do. Keep the change." He strolled away.

Dante never went back to the shoeshine stand, but the encounter left an indelible mark on his spirit, sparking his drive to build a real estate empire, one asset at a time.

The conversation also reminded him to be compassionate. Today, he gave back in many ways. Donating to the local shelter and food banks, which he frequented when he first arrived in the country. If not for them, he would've gone to bed hungry more often than not. He also spoke at local nonprofits to young people interested in entrepreneurship. In a city where one fourth of the population came from outside the United States, Dante hoped seeing him would inspire kids who looked like him and talked like him—and those who didn't—to reach for the stars.

The young woman returned with his Mercedes GLS SUV. He tipped her before sliding behind the wheel and pulled away from the curb.

The more he mulled the conversation with Annabelle, the more appealing her offer became. But he had sworn never to marry again. He liked his life and the freedom to come and go as he pleased, sleep with beautiful women, and answer to no one about anything. He certainly never considered remarrying the woman who had dumped him and trampled his heart in the process.

But Annabelle, the conniving wench, had planted a seed. He wanted that building. Not only was it prime commercial real estate, but it also had an interesting history. The original building was a fourteen-floor high-rise which had been demolished and replaced with the current seventy-six-story structure right before the Texas real estate collapse in the 1980s. For several years, there were no new major buildings built, which made the Hilderbrandt stand out and cemented its place as a landmark in Houston history—in a historical context as well as for its structural beauty.

If he gained possession of the plaza, it would be the crown jewel in his empire and declare he had truly arrived. He had won at life through hard work and perseverance—without an Ivy League education, three-piece suit, and *with* his accent. He imagined the day he signed the papers, essentially shooting two middle fingers at everyone who'd made him feel less than.

Dante eased to a stop at a red light, hardly noticing the other cars coming to a standstill around him.

If he agreed to Annabelle's ridiculous scheme, he had to be sure what he was getting himself into, and certain that no matter what happened during the course of their fake marriage, he obtained the proximity to Nolson that he needed. He couldn't trust her. But he had no doubt that if he got an audience with the man, he could convince Nolson to sell him the building.

He dialed Sebastian's number.

"Yes, Bossman?"

He smirked. They were more friends than boss and employee.

"I need you to do some research for me."

"Hang on, let me find something to write with. Where are you, anyway?"

"In the car."

"On the way home?" Sebastian asked, sounding surprised.

"Yes."

"I'm shocked. I can't believe Stella passed on the opportunity to sink her claws into you."

"She didn't. I was the one who passed. Do you have a pen?"

"Yes, I'm ready."

"Call around and see what you can find out about Hilderbrandt Enterprises. Are they really in financial trouble, and how bad is their situation? Be discreet."

"Not a problem."

"And find out what you can about all of Anna's lovers and boyfriends in the past five years."

Temporary silence.

"Er, what for? What do you plan to do with the information?" Sebastian finally asked.

"I want to know exactly how desperate my ex-wife is, if

indeed there is anyone else she's considering for the role of husband. I need all this information by Monday."

"Yes, sir."

They both hung up, and Dante rubbed his thumbnail along his lower lip. If there was no one else in the running, then he was in a much better position than expected. Information equaled power, and power would give him the upper hand when negotiating with his future wife.

$$\maltese \quad 5 \quad \maltese$$

You have a visitor. Dante Escarra is here to see you.

Annabelle's executive assistant had made that announcement five minutes ago, but she wasn't ready, pretending to be preoccupied while she girded her loins for the encounter with Dante.

She straightened her black sleeveless dress, which cinched at the waist and ruched at her hips. She checked her face in her compact. Her lips looked luscious in maroon lipstick, and her makeup was perfect. Calming an errant tendril of hair, she fixed a cool smile on her face. Her personal armor.

Stay positive, she thought.

Almost a week had passed since she walked into Dante's office. She'd been convinced his lack of communication was his way of letting her know he was *not* interested, but if he wasn't interested in her offer, he would have ignored her or communicated in a different way. His presence was a good sign. She hoped.

"Send him in."

Annabelle sat down and rested her arms on the rests of the leather executive chair as if she didn't have a care in the world, though her insides quivered with anticipation.

Dante strolled in, and to her chagrin, her breath caught. My goodness he was handsome, with almost-black brooding eyes and a hard, square jaw with angles sharp enough to cut marble.

His hair was cut close to his head, hiding the wavy pattern that appeared if he went too long between haircuts. Today he wore a black fitted jacket and white dress shirt unbuttoned at the top, silky black hairs peeking from beneath the cuffs. He didn't like ties. She'd practically had to beg him to wear one to their wedding ceremony the first time they married.

No one would ever know he was worth billions because he rarely wore three-piece suits, though the fine tailoring on his jacket and slacks indicated quality fabrics. He also didn't flaunt his wealth like many new money people did. He lived a surprisingly modest lifestyle, though she'd heard his home in Houston's prestigious River Oaks community had been decorated by one of the top interior designers in the country and looked spectacular inside and out.

"Ever heard of an appointment?" Annabelle asked by way of greeting.

"Why would I make an appointment when I know how desperate you are for an answer to your proposal?" he lobbed back.

"Yet here you are on a Thursday, when I asked for your answer by Monday."

"You should have known better than to give me an order."

Son of a bitch had made her wait just to make her sweat.

Annabelle forced out a little laugh. "Can I get you a drink?"

"No."

"Are you sure? I could fix one if you like."

"I wouldn't risk taking a drink from you. I might die on the way home."

Annabelle slapped her hand to her chest. "What a horrible thing to say. I need you, remember? I wouldn't kill you—right now." She smiled sweetly.

He studied her for a moment. "I came here to discuss your

proposal." Folding his large body onto the lavender Scandinavian sofa, he rested his ankle atop his knee and signaled with his hand that she should have a seat across from him.

Annabelle's fingers clenched the armrests. Who the hell did he think he was, ordering her around in her own office?

After a brief pause, she reluctantly rose from her chair and stalked over to the opposite sofa. Seated, she crossed one leg over the other, her body rigid and tense, noting with satisfaction when his eyes followed the movement. "I'm listening."

His gaze shifted upward. "I have decided to accept your proposal."

Annabelle released a slow breath, doing her best not to display her utter relief. "But?"

"What makes you think there is a but?"

"There's always a but."

Dante pulled lint from his black socks and smiled to himself, the dimple in each cheek making an appearance. "There is one thing."

I knew it. "What? Go ahead and tell me now. I can handle whatever curveball you have planned."

He rubbed his thumbnail across his lower lip—something he did whenever he was weighing options. "How soon would you like to get married?"

"As quickly as possible. I was thinking about May."

His dark eyebrows angled upward. "That's only two months away."

"Time is of the essence. My father is retiring in a few months, and I can't risk him handing the company to Albert Strong."

"And what about Nolson Hilderbrandt? How soon can you arrange a meeting with him after we're married? A week?"

Her eyebrows winged higher. "I can't *guarantee* a meeting within a week."

He dipped his head and looked at her in a penetrating way, expressing his displeasure without saying a word.

Annabelle took a deep breath. She couldn't afford to screw this up. "One week is impossible. The man is practically a recluse. He hardly ever leaves his estate and mostly works from home now, which I'm sure you know. I'll arrange a meeting as soon as I can."

"I hope you're not trying to play some foolish game with me. I expect you to do what you say, so a meeting with Nolson will be written into the contract. If the terms of the contract are not met, then the agreement is void. Don't think for one minute that because we will be married you can renege on your promise. Right now, I'm in an agreeable mood. You don't want me to become... disagreeable."

Annabelle swallowed. "Understood."

She knew very well how a 'disagreeable' Dante handled his foes. She had heard that one time a supplier tried to renegotiate their terms after he learned of the amount of money Dante would make off the project. He decided he'd bid too low and wanted a greater percentage of the revenue, so he purposely delayed the materials—causing a lock jam in the project's progress.

Of course, his behavior didn't sit well with her ex-husband. Delays meant money lost, which meant the charts and tables he loved to analyze would have to be redone and his margins would shrink. Rumor had it, Dante marched into the man's office *himself*, confronted him about the importance of keeping one's word, and used a technical violation in the contract to yank his business. Other companies followed when they learned what happened. The man went out of business in six months.

"I can probably get you an audience with him within a month of the wedding, but we get married *first*."

His eyes narrowed. He didn't like not being able to dictate the terms. "Understood."

"Every June, Nolson has a party at his estate," Annabelle continued. "Very short guest list, but Daddy and I always receive an invitation. As my husband, you'd automatically be able to attend. Does that suit you?"

Dante nodded, an inscrutable expression on his face. "Next, the prenup. It should be ironclad to protect us both. I don't want you trying to sink your claws into my company if yours collapses, and I'm sure you don't want me to use my vast resources to do a hostile takeover of yours."

His statement sounded like a warning. One of the reasons Dante was so successful was because of the amount of cash he had in reserve, available to leap on investment opportunities as they became available. He also had a stellar rating as a credit risk, which had banks clamoring to loan money for his business endeavors. Modest living had its benefits, and coming from a modest background meant he knew exactly where every nickel went and what the money was used for. During their marriage, his financial mind had been a beauty to behold—a lethal combination of business acumen and street smarts.

"I couldn't agree more. I'm glad we're both clear on how to proceed," Annabelle said evenly, though her stomach burned. When he left, she'd have to find an antacid to alleviate the pain.

"Now, to a more... delicate matter that I want to discuss with you," Dante continued. "Sex."

Tension burst into the room as the word dropped.

"Sex?"

"Yes, the thing people do when they're attracted to each other. In heterosexual relationships, the man places his penis in—"

"I know what sex is and how it's performed."

"I wasn't sure. You seemed confused."

"I'm not," Annabelle said in a hard voice.

"Good. I need to be able to release my built-up sexual frustration over the course of the marriage."

Of course. He had quite the sexual appetite.

Annabelle shrugged. "Fine. As I said before, be discreet."

"What about you? Don't you have needs?" His gaze crawled over her and lingered on her crossed legs.

She felt the weight of his stare as surely as if he'd touched her.

"Don't worry about me."

"*Ay Dio*s," he said softly. "Have all your rich boyfriends turned you off sex? You used to love it, or was that only with me?"

As her pulse raced, Annabelle forced a laugh. "And yet I left you."

"You didn't leave because the sex was bad, but because you couldn't handle sacrifice after growing up in the mansion on Lacewood Lane."

What he said was categorically untrue. She would've lived in a studio apartment the size of a shoebox with him. She left for a different reason, which she couldn't face without regret.

"What is the point of this conversation?" she asked in a sweet voice coated with ice.

"The point is, we both have a sexual appetite which must be satisfied during this one-year marriage. You know how cranky and irritable I can get."

She was well aware.

"I propose we agree to a schedule or a minimum number of times, to keep the frustration at bay."

Annabelle shrugged. "Sounds good to me. It's not a bad idea, actually. I'll need to release my frustrations, too. There are a few men I can call to scratch that particular itch. What kind of schedule did you have in mind?"

"You are not having sex with other men while you're married to me." Dante looked her dead in the eyes, unflinching.

Annabelle chuckled softly. "Oh really? You can have sex but I can't? How charming and so very... what's the word I'm looking for... 1950s of you. If I don't get to have sex, you don't either." She flashed her signature tight smile. "Final offer."

Then she waited, knowing full well what was at stake. She

only hoped he wanted the property more than he wanted to keep an imaginary chastity belt on her during the marriage.

"That is not going to work either. I propose sex at least one night per month."

Annabelle rolled her eyes. "Fine. One night per month. We can write it into the contract."

His eyes narrowed in a thoughtful way. "It's clear to me that you don't understand what I'm proposing. I want to have sex one night a month, Anna, with you."

6

W *ith you.*
The words rocked the room with the power of a 7.0-magnitude earthquake. Annabelle's pulse shot to life at the thought of being in his strong arms again. What the hell? Why couldn't she control her hormones around him? She hadn't lain next to him in ten freaking years, for heaven's sake.

"Excuse me?"

"You heard me. One night a month, with you, in my bed." Dante stretched both arms across the back of the sofa.

"I'd rather be bitten by a cobra."

"That can be arranged."

Annabelle laughed, a jagged sound of disbelief. "Our marriage will be sexless. *Un*consummated."

"No one can live under those conditions. We should have sex at least once a month. I would prefer it more often, but..." He shrugged.

Annabelle decided to humor him. "And how would that work exactly? Will we schedule intercourse on specific days?"

"No." He spoke calmly and with the nonchalance of a man discussing what he wanted to eat for dinner later. "Any night we choose."

"Randomly? So you intend to dangle the sex night over my head like a cudgel?"

She wouldn't know when or how he'd strike, but he could whenever he was ready, and she'd be at his mercy. This was a damn nightmare. She let out a humorless cackle of disbelief. When he didn't respond with even a stitch of amusement, her eyes widened.

"You're serious."

He stared at her with a stony expression. She was loath to be the first to speak, but she had to disabuse him of the notion that they would bump hips at any point during the 365 days they were married.

"Absolutely not." Annabelle shot to her feet and stalked to her desk.

"What are you afraid of?" he asked quietly behind her.

When she swung to face him again, a faint smirk lifted the corner of his mouth. How she hated that goddamn smirk. She itched to slap it off his *goddamn* face. "You're the last man on Earth I'd ever want to have sex with. Do you really want me to lie in bed with you, faking it?"

"You never faked it with me. Do you no longer enjoy sex? Did Alex and Reece and the others not satisfy you?" Dante asked with exaggerated concern.

She was shocked speechless for a moment. "You've done your homework."

"I know all about your ex-boyfriends and lovers, and I'm convinced none of them satisfied you the way I did."

Goodness, he was arrogant, and one hundred percent correct. Her toes curled with Dante, and she had no shame begging for his possession. She wished she could say her experience with other men had been the same.

"Unless you're planning to force me—"

"Please, *por favor*, I am not an animal."

"Then you're being unreasonable."

"Am I?" Rising slowly to his feet, Dante stood with his feet planted shoulder width apart. He tilted his head to the right. "You love sex as much, maybe more than I do. I still have the scars from you clawing my back." He rolled his shoulders as if reliving the moments.

He was exaggerating, but nonetheless, her face heated. "That's in the past."

"I need an answer, Anna."

She rubbed her sweaty palms together. "Why do you want to have sex with me? You could have any woman you want, and from what I've heard, you often do." She hoped the jealousy she felt didn't seep into her voice or her face.

"We both know sleeping with other people while we're in this pretend marriage is risky. We cannot risk the truth getting out."

He had a point, but it didn't mean she wanted to have sex with *him*. Scratch that. She apparently *did* want to have sex with him, but she preferred not to.

Everything about Dante screamed sex appeal. Midnight-black hair, angular face with high cheekbones and a solid, square jaw. He could charm the panties off a schoolmarm with his wicked, dimpled smile and the deep timbre of his accented voice.

"We are not having sex."

"You're sure?"

"Yes!" Annabelle snapped.

"You'll change your mind," he said with infuriating confidence.

"You're wrong."

"I'm never wrong."

She shot him her darkest scowl.

Her nerves were already frayed from this conversation. No way could she handle Dante touching and caressing her body. For the sake of self-preservation, she needed to keep distance between them. She had made too many mistakes when she was younger and fell in love too fast.

"All right. We'll take regularly scheduled sex off the table, hmmm? But you will want to have sex too. You said yourself you'll need someone to scratch your itch. When the day comes, I will be that someone. Your husband. No one else." He moved closer and his eyes bored into hers. "While we are married, our bodies belong to each other. I will not touch another woman, and you will not touch another man. You came to me with this proposition, and I will not budge on this stipulation. You might pretend you cannot imagine being in my arms again, but I look forward to having you in mine." His lustful gaze traveled the length of her body, clearly stripping her bare in his mind.

"I'm surprised you want me," she whispered.

"You should not be surprised. We always had chemistry, even during the last days of our marriage when we couldn't stand being in the same room together because of your lies."

"I didn't lie to you."

"No, you simply pretended to care about me and then ran off while I was working. Sneaking out of the apartment with all your possessions as if you were escaping from a monster." He said the last words through clenched teeth.

"I had to leave that way."

"Why?"

"Because I—because I didn't want you to try to convince me to stay. We weren't happy, and a clean break was best."

"*You* weren't happy. I thought I was working hard, providing for my wife, preparing a future for us together." Anger vibrated off him as he snarled the words.

"Is that what this is about? You want to have sex as some kind of revenge for leaving?"

"Revenge is the last thing on my mind. I want that building, and I'm willing to play your little game to get it. We need each other."

Annabelle swallowed. He was right, they did.

"As for your exes, if you want to maintain your friendships with them, fine, but make sure you don't embarrass me. There should be no suggestion of rekindling your romance with any of them."

"I could say the same to you about your legion of women."

"Legion is an exaggeration, but I promise not to embarrass you."

Dante tread closer and looked down into her face. "I'm a very patient man, Anna. I can wait until you come to me and beg me to pry your legs apart."

He stroked her jaw with the tip of one long finger. She froze, breath halted as he mesmerized her with his silky voice.

"You'll be waiting a very long time," she whispered huskily. She pushed at the wall of his chest.

He stepped back and licked his bottom lip, his dark, brooding eyes assessing her from head to toe. Her chest tightened and the inside of her thighs ached for the slide of his wet tongue. Could he see how much he had rattled her?

"I look forward to that night," Dante said, his voice raspy and low, holding her gaze for one long, charged moment. Finally, he started toward the door. "I will have my lawyer get in touch."

He walked out of the office, leaving the alluring scent of his cologne lingering in the air.

After the door closed, Annabelle pushed out a breath and rubbed the back of her neck under her thick hair. *What have I gotten myself into?*

To her horror, she felt dampness between her thighs, and her nipples tingled. Oh no, had he seen?

She glanced down at her dress, but her nipples weren't pressed against the fabric. Thank goodness they hadn't betrayed her.

She had run from this years ago. Back then, with very little to his name, Dante somehow managed to exude power. He overwhelmed. Now, he was more powerful. More overwhelming.

She wished there was another way to get what she wanted,

but she needed him. At least he needed her too. They were stuck together in a twisted bargain.

And she had been the one to initiate the deal with the devil.

7

Dante walked to the front door of the Buchanan mansion, located away from the hustle and bustle of the city. All the homes in the community were custom-built and two stories, on no fewer than three acres of land. Buchanan & Buchanan Properties had built most of the residences in the neighborhood years ago and developed the landscape by incorporating walking paths, a huge manmade lake, and a private golf course.

As he approached the door, he straightened the charcoal gray jacket he wore over a crisp white shirt. He'd thought about adding a tie but at the last moment changed his mind. At this stage of his life, no one would dare comment on his lack of neckwear.

He rang the doorbell and almost immediately was greeted by the female butler, Grace, an older Black woman with wrinkles at the corners of her eyes and a friendly, open face.

As in the past, she wore a uniform of gray pants and a gray shirt, her graying hair smoothed into a neat French roll.

"Hello, Mr. Escarra," she greeted him with a smile.

"Good evening, Grace, how are you?"

"I'm fine, thank you. I haven't seen you in a while."

Dante chuckled. "Yes, it has been awhile."

"You look well."

"So do you."

"I have a few more gray hairs, but I'm of sound mind and body." She opened the door wider, and he stepped across the threshold into the large entryway with an antique chandelier hanging from the high ceiling.

Grace clasped her hands in front of her. "I hear you and Annabelle are getting back together. Congratulations."

She watched him closely, her dark eyes sharp, alert, and assessing. She had worked for the Buchanans since Annabelle was a little girl, starting in the kitchen and moving up to the position of butler.

"Thank you."

"Love is funny, isn't it?"

"What do you mean?"

"Sometimes we're not ready for it. We don't know how to nurture it, take care of it, trust it. I do hope you're ready now." Her lips rested in a firm line.

Dante was about to speak when he caught movement at the corner of his eye.

Grace quietly slipped away, and Annabelle descended the staircase with a displeased expression on her face. He strolled toward her, taking stock of how the blue sleeveless dress emphasized her hourglass figure. He couldn't help but admire her body and the way her hair damn near sparkled under the light from the chandelier above.

She wore it half up, with half the strands pooling on her shoulders like silken black and honey-gold threads. He longed to drag his fingers through them, or better yet, wrap his fist in their softness and tug her head back for his demanding kiss.

All in due time...

At the bottom of the stairs, Annabelle lifted her head higher to glare at him. "You're late."

"I'm never late. Everyone else is early," Dante replied.

She rolled her eyes. "Let's get on with it. Daddy is in the great room reading. Oh, before I forget." She held out her left hand and showed off the engagement ring he'd given her eleven years ago.

Dante froze, his neck muscles tightening in shock. There wasn't much that left him speechless, but he was temporarily stunned into silence. Seeing the ring brought back a host of memories.

He had gone through the formality of asking Annabelle's father for her hand in marriage, but Clifton had been hesitant at first. He liked Dante well enough, though he didn't come from money and wasn't a member of their social class. He was concerned, however, that they were too young and moving too fast.

Dante hadn't wasted any time convincing him that he loved Annabelle and knew their marriage *would* last. How wrong he had been. Had he known, he would not have asked her to marry him only days later. The rented hotel room he had chosen for their weekend away had rose petals strewn on the floor and candles filled the air with the scents of vanilla and lavender.

In the flickering candlelight, he lowered to one knee and presented her with a princess-cut diamond ring on a gold band. Other than the single piece of property he owned, it was the most expensive item he had ever purchased.

The expense had been negligible when he saw the wide-eyed excitement on her face, and she said the one word he'd hoped to hear—*Yes.*

"I'm shocked you kept that ring. I assumed you threw it away, or perhaps sold it to buy something you appreciated more."

"Believe me, I considered doing something like that, but I decided to hold on to it—as a sort of reminder, to make sure I didn't make the same mistake again." She spoke in a low voice and kept her eyes lowered to her fingers so he couldn't read her expression.

"And yet here you are," Dante said in a hard voice.

Lifting her head, her face was cool and expressionless. "I have a goal this time. One year, and I get what I want. We both do."

She swung away, but before she could take a step, Dante grabbed her hand.

She stared at him with wide eyes. "What are you doing?"

She tried to pull away, but his fingers tightened, and he moved closer.

Annabelle stood firm, defiant, as if daring him to attack. He only knew she was agitated by the accelerated speed of the pulse at the base of her throat.

"If we're going to act like we're in love, holding hands will help us look the part," Dante explained evenly.

She opened her mouth as if to protest, then thought better of it, and released a breath. "Fine," she muttered, clearly displeased.

He loosened the tight grip on her soft fingers. "You should also try putting a smile on your face and acting as if you're happy to see me."

A fake, tight smile lifted the corners of her mouth.

"You can do better than that. Remember what is at stake," Dante admonished.

"Believe me, I haven't forgotten." She took a deep breath, and then a genuine smile appeared on her lips. "Better?"

"*Mucho mejor*. Much better."

Hand in hand, they walked to the back of the house and entered the great room, where a two-story ceiling made the already large space appear larger. Windows along the back wall showed the lit grounds at the rear of the property.

"Daddy, look who has arrived," Annabelle said with believably manufactured excitement.

She was a better actress than Dante expected. Had he not seen her real reaction seconds ago, he would actually believe she was happy to see him.

Clifton Buchanan sat in a recliner with glasses perched on his nose as he read his iPad. In his mid-sixties, gray in his hair, and a fully white beard, Clifton was the epitome of culture and money in chinos, a dress shirt and tie, and a sweater thrown over the ensemble. The minute he saw them, his face broke into a smile.

"Dante!" Removing his glasses, he came immediately to his feet and tossed the tablet on the recliner.

"Clifton." Dante extended a hand.

"I never thought I'd see you in this house again," Clifton said with a laugh, clasping Dante's hand in both of his and giving a vigorous shake.

"I never thought I'd be in this house again. Good to see you."

"How are you?"

"Better since Annabelle and I have reconciled." Dante slipped an arm around her waist, and she stiffened.

"I have to admit, I was very surprised when Annabelle told me, but I couldn't be happier. I was disappointed when the two of you divorced. But you've made good use of the time since you've been apart, building a successful business. Please, have a seat." Clifton waved a hand in the direction of the L-shaped sofa across from his recliner.

Dante and Annabelle sat down beside each other, and she looped an arm through his. As she leaned her soft body into his side, his lungs filled with the scent of orange blossoms and sweet jasmine, and his loins came alive with sudden hunger.

Grace entered the room with a tray containing three glasses of iced tea and homemade sugar cookies. She served Clifton first, who thanked her, and then handed glasses of tea to Dante and Annabelle. She placed the plate of cookies on the table in front of the couple and left the room as quietly as she entered.

"Those cookies are delicious, but I'm not allowed to have any," Clifton said, eyeing the one Annabelle lifted to her lips.

"Doctor's orders," she explained. "Grace and I make sure he follows them."

"What would we do without the women in our lives? This is unsweetened tea." Taking a sip, Clifton relaxed into the recliner.

"How did the two of you reconcile? Annie insisted on waiting until you were here together to tell me the story."

They had spent an hour the day before discussing an explanation. Dante sipped his tea and let Annabelle take the lead in the lying.

"We both ended up in the Bank of Houston elevator alone and were forced to have a conversation," she began.

Later they ran into each other again at a restaurant down the street from the bank, and Dante asked if he could join her. Sparks flew from there, especially when they started reminiscing about the past. They exchanged numbers and began seeing each other in secret, in case the relationship didn't work. A perfectly believable story, though not one iota of it was true.

When she finished, her father smiled at them both. "I can't tell you how happy I am the two of you are getting back together. It's never too late to rectify a wrong, and you're still young. Do you have plans for an engagement party?"

"No. We aren't planning to have one," Annabelle answered.

Her father frowned. "You didn't have one the first time. I think it would be a great idea to have an engagement party this time. I can't have my daughter marry the great Dante Escarra—the most sought after man in all of Houston—without announcing it to the world."

"It would have to be on very short notice. Within a few weeks."

"Why so soon? Have you picked a date for the wedding yet?"

"Yes, May sixteenth."

Clifton's eyebrows raised higher. "So soon."

Dante took Annabelle's hand. "We didn't see the point in waiting. We've lost so much time already."

Clifton nodded. "True, true. Then we need to move swiftly on the engagement party. It's a yes on the engagement party, right, honey?"

"I, uh—yes."

"Perfect. Now that's settled, do you mind checking on

dinner? I want to talk to Dante alone for a bit. Would you join me in my study for a pre-dinner cognac and cigar?" Clifton rose from his chair.

"I would love to." Dante and Annabelle stood, and he dropped a kiss on her pillowy soft cheek. He heard her soft inhale, right before he withdrew.

He followed Clifton toward the door leading into his private study.

Before they entered, he glanced over his shoulder and caught an expression on Annabelle's face, but it quickly disappeared. What was that look?

If he didn't know better, he'd say it was pain. He suddenly remembered a past conversation with Annabelle about her father and how her brother's untimely death had left a void— one she had tried unsuccessfully to fill.

He opened his mouth to suggest she join them in the study, but she spoke first.

"I'll call you when dinner is ready." She left the room without another word.

Dante stared after her, an odd emotion sweeping through his chest.

"Dante, are you ready?"

"Right behind you."

8

Annabelle parked her car in the driveway behind a huge white catering van. The front door was open, and servers dressed in white jackets and black slacks ferried covered containers of food indoors. Meanwhile, other workers wheeled tables and stacked chairs around the side of the house destined for the backyard where the engagement party was scheduled to unfold in several hours.

Inside, Grace directed traffic to the kitchen, where Annabelle was certain their chef and other household staff waited. She smiled at Grace, and the older woman acknowledged her with a quick nod before her attention was taken by a young man wheeling in a cart filled with a variety of liquors.

Annabelle ran up the winding staircase and left them to their tasks. She had her own to accomplish.

The past few weeks had passed in a blur of planning for the party and the wedding. She had seen Dante only twice in that period, and one of those times had been on a video call to discuss the final numbers for the guest list. He had been out of town all week, leaving her to finalize the details for their engagement party. Granted, this whole charade was her idea, but she was miffed by his lack of interest.

Her father, on the other hand, was very involved and had injected his wishes regarding the engagement party guest list and other areas—including the catering company—which belonged to a longtime friend of his. Because of his involvement, the small gathering of guests she'd wanted had ballooned beyond close friends and family to include business associates and more people in his circle than hers. All because her father was excited to have the great Dante Escarra back in his family, and he wanted the world to know.

When she pushed open the door to her bedroom, her best friend Lacey was already there, seated in an overstuffed chair in front of the duvet-covered bed, legs propped on an ottoman. When Annabelle entered, she looked up from her phone.

"There you are. I was about to call you," her friend said.

"I had to make a stop on the way home, and then I got stuck in traffic."

Annabelle crossed the white carpet to her vintage makeup vanity. The stylish furniture was gold and seafoam-green, its colors blending well with the pastel decor of her bedroom. On top, she displayed a collection of vintage perfume bottles in a bejeweled vanity tray. These were her favorite ones, but the rest of the collection resided on built-in shelves in the closet.

She placed her purse on the vanity and turned to face her friend. "What are you doing here so early?"

"I came to see if you needed help."

Lacey was tall and svelte with porcelain skin and a very short blonde pixie cut. She had modeled for a few years but discovered she enjoyed designing clothes more than she liked walking the runway in them. Her parents, however, had not been excited about yet another of her entrepreneurial ideas and refused to finance her designer aspirations. If she wanted to be successful, she had to succeed on her own.

Annabelle wholeheartedly supported her friend. Some people took a little longer to figure out what they wanted to do with their lives. The same had happened to her. Her friend needed support, not criticism.

"I'm fine. I'm going to take a long soak in the tub. Rocky and Clari will be here in an hour to help me get ready," she said, referring to her makeup artist and his hair stylist wife. They worked as a team, and she always called them for major events when she wanted to look her best.

Lacey bit the corner of her lip, a frown creasing her brow.

"What's that look on your face?" Annabelle asked, placing a hand on her hip.

"Hear me out. I know we've talked about this before, but *are you sure?* There's no other way to convince your father to recommend you as CEO to the board?"

Annabelle released an exaggerated sigh. "Believe me, if there was, I would jump at the chance. I wouldn't have approached Dante about getting married if I wasn't absolutely certain there was no other way to take control of Daddy's company. Do you think I *want* to do this? My father will only consider letting me take over if he believes I'll be able to consult with Dante. Otherwise, he'd rather merge with Albert's firm and let him take charge. Daddy is loyal to him because... well, he's a loyal person. He believed Albert when he said there would be no layoffs and the company will remain the same. I know that's not true. Not only will there be layoffs, but the entire culture of the company will change."

"Albert has known your father a long time and expects the merger to take place. If it doesn't, who knows what he might do."

Annabelle had thought about his reaction, but she could handle Albert. "What can he do? Nothing. Once my father recommends me to the board—which I'm confident will happen —Albert can forget about becoming CEO of the merged companies. Plain and simple. I went to college, earned my degree, and put in five years at my *family's* company. I deserve the opportunity to run Buchanan & Buchanan."

If her brother were alive, there would be no question that he'd take over. It had been expected and welcomed. Why should things be different for Annabelle? She was Clifton's only heir, and as chief development officer, she was responsible for land acquisition, project design, and construction planning. She had growth plans already sketched out for her father's firm. He only had to give her a chance.

Lacey's eyes turned sympathetic. "I'm not denying you've worked hard, but I'm worried you can't stop Albert."

Annabelle shrugged, dismissing her friend's concern. "There's nothing he can do. The bottom line is, Dante and I are going to get married very soon, and then Daddy will talk to the board. They listen to what he says, so I'll become the new CEO. The end."

An amused smile softened Lacey's lips. "Well, you certainly have everyone talking. You're all over the blogs and society pages. When you came in, I was reading the latest on *Houston Society's* online magazine. They devoted an *entire* column to you and Dante."

Annabelle groaned, dropping onto the cushioned stool of her vanity. She shouldn't be surprised. *Houston Society* pretended they were a classy magazine, but they were nothing more than a tabloid with zero journalistic integrity. They catered to readers who gorged on details of the controversies afflicting local celebrities and politicians and relished every misstep in the public eye.

"Who wrote the article?" she asked with trepidation.

"Tina Mae."

Double groan. That horrible woman was the worst one, and after they had a run-in years before, she and Annabelle had a hate-hate relationship. Tina was like a vulture who circled the carcasses of prominent personalities for clicks on a website. Annabelle couldn't stand her and dreaded knowing what she'd written.

"What did she say?"

Lacey looked down at her phone. "The headline reads: Dante Escarra and Annabelle Buchanan Are Back Together, But Will The Relationship Last?" She paused. "Do you want me to continue?"

Annabelle placed a tight-lipped smile on her face. "Yes," she replied, though irritation clogged her throat and threatened to suffocate her.

Her friend continued. "Dante Escarra, Houston's top commercial real estate developer, might soon be taken off the market by none other than the princess of Buchanan & Buchanan Properties, his ex-wife, Annabelle Buchanan. The couple tied the knot in their early twenties but went their separate ways after a brief marriage. Now, ten years later, they're back together. When the oh-so-hot-and-spicy Dante—"

"Really? Did she have to say all that?"

"You know how she is," Lacey said with a one-shoulder shrug. "When the oh-so-hot-and-spicy Dante isn't crushing his competition in commercial real estate, he's wining and dining his way between the thighs of some of the most glamorous women in the country."

"Oh my goodness!" Annabelle exclaimed.

Lacey grimaced. "I know. She's horrible. Let me skip some of this. Um, let's see... Oh, here we go. She talks about the engagement party: This very weekend, the couple is throwing an engagement party to announce to the world that they're giving love another chance. We don't know why the couple divorced the first time, but it seems they haven't lost that loving feeling. Will the relationship last? Only time will tell, but we sincerely hope they aren't destined for another heartbreak. The—"

"Enough." Annabelle rubbed her temple.

"You're missing the best part, though it's not great."

"I don't think I want to hear anymore."

"Trust me, you want to hear this."

Annabelle blew out a breath and then motioned for her friend to continue.

Lacey cleared her throat. "Could it be Princess Annabelle regrets her past decision? After all, Señor Escarra is a billionaire now, worth more than he was when they originally married and more than she is now."

"I should sue that bitch," Annabelle muttered.

The first time she and Dante married, the magazine took great pleasure in pointing out their financial differences. At the time, Dante owned one property—a three-bedroom home he lived in with five other men. No one thought he deserved her, and there were whispers of her marrying down. How ironic the same media was now suggesting *she* was the one marrying for money.

Lacey put her phone in her purse. "What happens in a year when you divorce Dante? There's going to be a scandal, and of course Tina Mae will be leading the charge to dissect your second divorce. Not to mention, your father will be disappointed."

Annabelle crossed her arms. "I don't care what other people think. As for my father, he'll be so impressed by my performance at the company, losing Dante as a son-in-law won't matter."

"I hope you're right. I hate being a Negative Nellie right now, but I have to ask this last question. Aren't you worried Dante might try to double-cross you?"

A burst of laughter escaped Annabelle's lips. "*Of course.* I know my husband, and he can't be trusted. We agreed to sign a prenuptial agreement, which includes him never getting his grubby hands on my company." She swiveled on the stool and examined her face in the large round mirror on the vanity. She should have gotten a facial but didn't have time in between running errands today.

"*Ex*," Lacey said behind her.

"What?" Annabelle frowned at her friend in the mirror.

"Ex-husband." Lacey arched an eyebrow.

"What did I say?"

"You said 'husband.'"

"Oh." Annabelle shrugged. "Slip of the tongue."

"Mhmm."

She ignored whatever Lacey was trying to imply by her response and continued examining her skin.

"I better get out of here," Lacey said, rising to her feet, "so I can get ready in time to come back for the festivities. I'll see you later."

"Bye."

Annabelle sat for a few minutes longer, thinking about how she'd mistakenly used the word "husband." No big deal. Dante *was* almost her husband, so it was only natural she referred to him as such.

She filled the tub with her favorite bath tonic, which contained Himalayan salts and lavender. Sinking into the warm water, she pushed aside thoughts of Dante and envisioned the day she'd stand behind the desk in her father's office, in charge of all their properties and developing new ones. The same people who'd worked at the company for years would be standing right beside her.

The growth plan she'd sketched out needed tweaking, but she'd worked on the idea for over a year and was very confident once she took charge, implementing the necessary changes would propel the company into further prosperity.

Opening her eyes, Annabelle tilted her head back and stared up at the ceiling. Did loved ones who'd passed really keep track of what was happening in the present world? She didn't believe so, but skepticism didn't stop her from hoping that by this time next year her mother and brother would be proud of her accomplishments.

9

By the time Annabelle finished her bath, she was relaxed and serene, confident nothing that happened tonight could upset or throw her off-kilter.

Wrapped in a rose gold silk robe and matching fuzzy slippers, she entered her walk-in closet and examined her Oscar de la Renta dress. The gorgeous gown's appearance made everything more real, and her heart tightened with fear or anticipation, she wasn't sure which.

A knock sounded on the bedroom door.

"Come in," she called.

Rocky entered with a large makeup case and a bag. He looked more like a tattoo artist than a makeup artist, with two sleeves of tattoos running up his bare arms, spiky black hair, and a ring in his nose. The hair stylist, his wife Clari, wheeled in her supplies behind him. Annabelle had never seen Clari wear her blonde hair in any other style than the layered bob she currently wore, but the woman was a magician when it came to styling.

"Are you ready for us?" Rocky asked.

Annabelle nodded, sliding onto the seat at the vanity and locking eyes with him. "Definitely. Work your magic. I want their mouths to fall open when I walk into the party."

❦

MUCH LATER, AFTER ROCKY AND CLARI FINISHED AND GUESTS started arriving, Annabelle remained alone in her room anxiously pacing as she waited for Dante to arrive.

She stopped for a minute and observed her appearance in the full-length mirror. The designer dress looked amazing on her. The halter top of white organza fit close over her torso, highlighting her waistline and full breasts. Meanwhile, the skirt was made of the softest black velvet. The sharp contrast of the colors gave her a polished, elegant appearance.

When Rocky had seen her, he whistled. "You look fabulous, as usual."

And she felt fabulous. No matter the reason for tonight's party, she looked damn good. When she looked good, she was confident. Confidence could carry her through the night and the weeks until the wedding, particularly when people like that witch Tina Mae took shots at her.

She posed in the mirror, practicing different versions of her smile and checking out her back as she cast a glance over one shoulder. She'd definitely want a photo taken in that position.

She checked the time on her phone again.

Where the hell was Dante? Of all the days to be late, why did he choose to be late to their engagement party—their formal debut as a reunited couple?

Or maybe he wasn't coming?

Oh no. She hadn't considered the possibility of him not showing up. She hadn't talked to him all week.

Annabelle snatched up her phone to call him, but it rang instead. "Yes?"

"Mr. Escarra has arrived and is waiting for you in the foyer," a staff member said.

She clutched her chest with relief and berated herself for that moment of panic. "Tell him I'll be right there."

Taking a deep breath, she double-checked her appearance.

Dabbing a little more lipstick on her lips, she rubbed them together to evenly distribute the color. Then she smoothed damp hands over her full skirt.

Why was she nervous? She looked incredible.

Rocky had applied makeup that gave her a minimalist look, adding bronzer to make her skin shimmer, which was perfect for the fading light as the sun set. As for her hair, it was styled in stacked double buns and loose tendrils allowed to casually frame her face. She'd chosen diamond earrings and a diamond bracelet for her right wrist.

She released a controlled exhale. "Show time."

At the top of the staircase, she looked down and saw Dante waiting near the door with his back to her, one hand casually tucked into his pocket as he surveyed the outdoors. As her heel hit the top stair, he slowly turned, and her breath caught. Holding on to the railing, she paused and remained motionless. The air stilled in the cavernous foyer. He walked toward her, moving as if in slow motion in a white shirt, charcoal jacket, and charcoal slacks.

Annabelle continued her descent, unable to read his expression, but her heart raced with each step that brought them closer. "You look nice."

A freaking understatement if there ever was one.

Dante rarely wore suits. If his face wasn't known throughout Houston, one would take him for an average middle-class guy. Not a real estate mogul with offices in three cities and thousands of people under his employ. Tonight's clothing choice was simple, yet she knew without seeing the rest of the guests that he had outdressed every man in attendance.

When her feet finally touched the marble tile at the bottom of the staircase, Dante took her hand. At first, she thought he was about to kiss her fingers, but instead, he simply held her and examined her from top to bottom.

"*Mi reina*," he said in a mocking tone. My queen.

"Don't call me that."

"I'll call you whatever I damn well please." He dropped a fleeting kiss to her cheek.

At the touch of his warm lips, heat flared on her skin. Annabelle lowered her gaze to hide the reaction and swallowed hard. The *thump, thump, thump* of her heart was so loud she worried he might hear the sound.

Something was happening to her. Something she couldn't quite control. Her body was hot and her heart raced.

She cleared her throat. "Are you ready?"

"Before we meet our guests, I have something for you."

She cast a wary look at him as he reached into his pocket and removed a sapphire-blue box. He opened it and revealed an Asscher-cut diamond ring. The size and clarity of the stone stole her breath. It had to be at least five carats and was flanked on two sides by equally brilliant white diamonds affixed to a platinum band.

"Give me your hand, Anna."

She let him take her hand, and he removed the smaller ring and placed the Asscher-cut diamond on her finger.

"I promised you a bigger ring, and now I can afford to give you one," he said quietly. He stared at her manicured hands, his jaw tight.

She remembered the night he asked her to marry him as vividly as if the proposal occurred the day before. She hadn't cared about the size of the ring. She'd been so excited because she loved him.

"I love it," Annabelle whispered.

"One day, I'll buy you a bigger one."

"No." She spread her fingers and eyed the ring with a happy, satisfied smile. "This is the only one I want. The one I'll keep forever."

"Now you have a ring worthy of a queen. *Mi reina.*"

His words saddened her. He had no idea she had truly been satisfied with the smaller diamond.

What else had he been mistaken about?

Dante tucked her hand in his arm, and they walked through

the house. The old Dante had calloused hands from toiling as a day laborer. The rough texture was long gone, and his skin was smooth to the touch.

Her knees trembled but gained strength as they walked. A member of the staff greeted them with a smile and then swung open the French doors.

"Mr. Dante Escarra and Ms. Annabelle Buchanan have arrived," he announced to the waiting group.

All heads turned in their direction, and the gathered guests clapped as they made their grand entrance onto the back lawn. Annabelle smiled at the visitors, including a few members of the press who she recognized.

Time to sell this engagement, she thought, walking forward to greet the guests.

The catering company had done a stellar job. Overhead lights were strung from poles, and battery-operated lanterns formed a perimeter to enclose the invitees. Tables were draped in delicate white linens, arranged so small groups could have intimate conversations while they enjoyed the outdoors. Several long tables contained crystal serving dishes filled with heavy hors d'oeuvres and were adorned with floral arrangements in bright summer colors.

Annabelle and Dante spent the evening circulating among the guests, separately and together. Each time someone said "Congratulations" or "Glad you found your way back to each other," she nodded and smiled and thanked them. She did that often, until her cheeks began to hurt.

Because she kept busy with the guests, she didn't have time to eat, and after a couple of hours, her stomach started a quiet growl. Departing from a conversation with Lacey and one of her out-of-town cousins, she went to one of the tables and made a small plate of chicken meatballs, added a tostada topped with spicy shrimp and mango salsa, and squeezed on a grilled cauliflower taco with jicama-carrot slaw.

She made her way over to the beverage station to order one

of the signature drinks. "I'll take a raspberry and pomegranate cocktail, please," she said to the young woman behind the counter.

She mixed the drink and handed Annabelle a glass filled with purple liquid. Taking a grateful sip of the fruity beverage, her sigh of satisfaction was cut short when a broad-shouldered blond came into her line of sight.

"Annabelle." Sebastian's voice was cool as he took a bottle of beer from the tub of ice.

"Sebastian," she said, her voice equally frosty.

That was the best either of them could do by way of a greeting. Sebastian didn't care for her and was very protective of Dante—as if the devil needed protecting.

Sebastian had distrusted her from the start and harbored suspicions that she was a pampered socialite princess using Dante to explore life outside her socio-economic circle. He assumed when the fascination with a working-class man ended, she'd return to the life she knew and preferred. When she left Dante, he must have believed his suspicions about her were confirmed.

He and Dante met in a unique way. Dante found Sebastian sleeping in his car near Dante's house. His parents had kicked him out in a bizarre effort to force him to be independent. Dante knew what it was like to struggle and be homeless, and he sympathized with Sebastian's situation. He offered him a room in the first property he purchased—a small place with three bedrooms, but he ran it like a boarding house with a total of four other roommates.

The two became good friends and remained close over the years. When Dante got married, Sebastian was his best man. As he built his empire, Sebastian worked with him. Their loyalty to each other was unshakeable.

"Is Elise here?" she asked, referring to his live-in girlfriend Dante had told her about.

"She went to visit her parents for the weekend."

"Oh."

They both stood awkwardly for a moment, neither knowing what to say next. She nibbled a chicken meatball, and he seemed to have forgotten the beer in his hand as he surveyed the gathered crowd.

Annabelle shot him a curt smile. "Well, I—"

Her father tapped a knife against an empty glass. "Can I have your attention, please? Just for a few minutes. Annie, Dante, please join me."

Annabelle stifled a sigh. Oh well, so much for satisfying her hunger.

✥ 10 ✥

Setting down her food, Annabelle joined Dante to the right of her father.

"I won't take too much time, but before everyone leaves, I wanted to say a few words." Clifton clasped his hands together. "I'm happy to have you all here tonight to celebrate the upcoming marriage of my lovely daughter, Annabelle, and her future husband, Dante Escarra. As many of you know, they were married a long time ago, much younger and in my opinion, perhaps not ready for all that marriage entailed at the time. When they separated, I was heartbroken. I had lost another son."

Empathetic murmurs filled the room.

"But they're back together again, and I must say I'm a very happy man. I believe this time their marriage will last because they've both grown and experienced life. Dante, welcome back to the family. I hope you stay for good this time."

Laughter and a chorus of "Here, here!" filled the space.

A twinge of guilt filled Annabelle's chest. She didn't like deceiving her father, but there was no better way to accomplish her goals.

"I would like to say a few words."

Her head snapped up at the sound of Dante's voice.

He extended a hand. Widening her smile, Annabelle placed her hand in his warm clasp.

"What are you doing?" she asked from the corner of her mouth.

Instead of answering, he gazed at her with loving eyes, assuredly fooling everyone there except her.

"This is completely unplanned, but I feel as if it's necessary. I arrived in this country fifteen years ago at the age of seventeen, searching for the American dream. Years later, I met this beautiful woman and was welcomed into her family. As Clifton said, perhaps Anna and I were too young at the time. I consider myself a very lucky man to have won her heart again. This time, I plan to keep it."

Without warning, he dipped her over his arm—like a scene out of a 1950s romantic film—and stunned her with a kiss. Camera flashes went off, and cheers and whistles erupted in the night.

His warm hand splayed across her back in support, and his tongue eased apart her lips. The fiery heat of passion and desire rushed through her veins, and liquid heat pooled between her thighs, making her core *ache*.

Her heart raced. Her knees softened. With a faint whimper, Annabelle curled both arms around the back of Dante's neck and devoured him in kind, reveling in the firm texture of chest muscles pressed against her soft breasts and making her nipples pebble into hard points.

Finally, Dante released her lips and straightened, and Annabelle's heart pounded in her chest. She couldn't believe he had kissed her. She couldn't believe she had reacted with such unfettered enthusiasm.

She smiled at the assembled crowd, her head swimming and her breathing coming in short, sharp spurts. She never denied Dante was still very attractive, but she hadn't expected to react to him in that way.

Oh shit. She was in trouble.

❦

ANNABELLE STORMED THROUGH HER BEDROOM DOOR SEVERAL paces ahead of Dante.

The guests had left, and the kiss had taken place over an hour ago, but she was still fuming. Angry at him and angry at herself. She couldn't believe she had kissed him back and, despite a hoard of onlookers, thoroughly enjoyed the way he'd devoured her lips.

Dante sauntered in after her, a lazy smile fixed at the corner of his mouth. Normally she wasn't a violent person, but she itched to smack the expression off his face.

She kicked off her shoes. "You had no right to kiss me earlier," she hissed.

"The guests enjoyed it, and there will be some great photos for the local media. You should be thanking me. The kiss should keep people from questioning the reason we reunited."

"It wasn't part of the plan. Moving forward, keep your lips to yourself!"

She took off for the walk-in closet but didn't get far before Dante somehow crossed the room and grabbed her arm, yanking her around to face him.

The lazy humor was gone. Anger had taken its place and blazed down at her from his eyes.

"Let us get one thing straight, shall we? You do not tell me what to do. We talk. We discuss. We negotiate. We come to a mutual agreement."

She stepped back and pulled out of his warm grip. "A mutual agreement? That hasn't happened at all in recent weeks. I've had to make virtually every decision concerning the engagement party and the wedding by myself because you're either too busy or—let's be honest—not interested."

"You were the one who came up with the idea to remarry," he reminded her in an even tone.

"That doesn't mean I have to do everything alone!" Annabelle snapped.

Resentment swelled in her chest. Not once had he asked how the plans were going or if she needed help.

He left everything up to her, which was much different from the first time they had married. Back then, he'd been very involved. They planned every minute of the ceremony and reception together, and though some of the tasks were obviously mundane to him, he'd participated all along the way.

This time around, while she fussed over seating charts, flowers, and decorations, Dante was nowhere to be found, carrying on as if he wasn't getting married in mere weeks. His disinterest chafed, and having to do everything herself was nerve-racking and annoying. As if she was the only one getting married.

"I assumed that's the way you wanted things. You're a bit of a control freak, whether you want to admit it or not."

Her eyes narrowed. "Talk about the pot calling the kettle black. All the more reason why we should have discussed *the kiss,* which we didn't." She shook with rage and... something else.

An unquenched need. A desire to kiss that cruel mouth of his again. To have his large hands on her bare skin and his firm lips against hers, making intimate parts of her body quiver with longing. She craved him and wanted him to slam her against the wall and force his thighs between hers.

Heat flushed her cheeks as she fought the sexy thoughts from taking over.

"That was a spur-of-the-moment decision, and in the future, we will discuss the kisses," Dante said calmly.

"*There will be no more kisses,*" Annabelle said, placing extra emphasis on each word. She couldn't afford to have these feelings come to the surface again. Complicated feelings of lust, anger, and affection.

"There will be more kisses," Dante said with alarming confidence.

"Are you threatening me?"

"Not at all, but we both know what will happen when we have to live together in the same house and share a bed."

She blinked, temporarily shocked. "Excuse me? Share a bed? We never said—"

"How do you plan to convince people our marriage is real if we're not sleeping in the same bed?"

"Don't you have your staff sign NDAs?"

"Of course, but there's no guarantee they will adhere to those agreements. We must be smart. Besides, after that kiss, I don't think we'll have any problem rekindling the passion between us, do you? We have something to look forward to. We'll both enjoy it, like we used to." His gaze dipped to the bodice of her dress, and her traitorous nipples tightened.

"You wish."

Dante stepped closer and studied her with a slight head tilt and narrowed eyes. "You pretend you don't want me, but we both know you do. Your body betrays you, *querida*. You kissed me like a woman who enjoyed the contact. If I place my hand between your legs right now, will you be wet for me?"

Annabelle drew in a sharp breath. "Go to hell."

A self-satisfied smirk teased his lips and made his dimples appear. "I want you. I can admit I do, though I am disgusted with myself. You may have faked your love for me when we were married, but you never faked your desire, and I can't wait to satisfy—"

Annabelle stepped back and glared at him. "If you entered into this agreement thinking you'd be allowed back into my bed, you're in for a huge disappointment. The only thing you can expect to receive from our marriage is contact with Nolson Hilderbrandt. That's it."

He laughed. "You don't like the truth, eh?"

"What I don't like is you talking to me as if you know my

mind. I will never have sex with you again. Why can't you accept that?"

He shrugged. "I don't believe you. We will be married for a year, and neither of us will be able to sleep with other people. We both have desires. Needs. You will change your mind."

This son of a...

Annabelle slammed her hands on her hips. "No, I won't. Furthermore, we will not share a bed. That's not part of the agreement. Since you agree I'm the one running this farce of a marriage, make sure you follow these instructions. I want my own bedroom. Talk to your staff or do whatever you need to. We have to share a home, but I will *not* share a bed with you."

He rubbed his thumb across his lower lip, his eyes becoming hooded as his gaze took yet another leisurely stroll down her body. His review was obscenely thorough. "You will cry out my name the way you did when we were married before. I used to worry everyone in the building could hear your screams. Do you remember?"

Of course she remembered. The laughter and camaraderie had fizzled, but their physical need for each other had remained unmatched. Dante was probably an even more skilled lover than he was before. In all these years, no other man had made her feel the way he did, but she'd die before admitting as much to him.

With a haughty lift to her chin, Annabelle responded to the question. "No, I don't."

He smiled again, flashing perfect teeth at her. "*Mentirosa.*"

Translation: *Liar.*

"See yourself out."

"As you wish, *mi reina.*" With a mocking bow and a wicked laugh, Dante strolled out of the bedroom.

A nnabelle returned from lunch with her father, her belly full and carrying a container of leftovers. The next quarterly board meeting was taking place six weeks after her wedding. He hadn't given any indication that his position about Albert had changed, but she was hopeful.

She placed the food in her office refrigerator and picked up one of the framed photos from her desk. A picture of her and Clifton Jr. The last one they'd taken together before his untimely death. Because they had different mothers, he was a blond-haired replica of their father. In the photo, he and Annabelle were beside the pool, and her mother had taken the shot. They were both grinning and flashing the peace sign.

Annabelle smiled faintly, her heart squeezing tight with the pain of missing him. Nineteen years and the twinge of pain never failed to resurrect at thoughts of him. Both he and her mother had been taken too soon.

"I'm going to succeed, Cliffy, like you would have. Just watch. You'll be proud of me," Annabelle whispered.

She replaced the frame on her desk and went to one of the file cabinets. Pretty soon, there wouldn't be a need for the cabinet. She had convinced her father to go paperless and had started the transition herself. When she became CEO, she was going to institute a paperless policy for the entire company.

She removed the document she needed and walked slowly to her desk, head bent over the file.

"You haven't won yet."

The statement came from behind her, and Annabelle swung around, coming face to face with Albert Strong. He stood in the open doorway of her office with one hand casually tucked into the pocket of his pants.

What is he *doing here?*

At fifty-five, Albert had a few strands of gray in his black hair, right above his forehead, and the beginnings of crow's feet hung at the corners of his eyes. Though he was fit and moderately attractive, she considered him ugly on the inside. His plans for the company soured her stomach, and his lying to her father about his plans enraged her.

Turning her back to him, she refastened her attention on the report she had been reviewing before his arrival. "I don't know what you mean. I'm not playing a game."

She sensed, rather than heard him walk deeper into the room.

"You know exactly what I mean."

He was way too close. So close she was surprised his breath didn't brush the back of her neck. Tossing the document on her desk, she sidestepped him and put distance between them. Resting her hands on her hips, she stared him down.

"Was there something you needed? I don't have time to talk in riddles."

"Your father is not going to turn over the company to you."

Anger bubbled inside her. "And why do you say that, Albert? Because you purposely ingratiated yourself with him and assumed the merger was a done deal? Unless you have something in writing, he has the right to change his mind."

"This company is mine," he said in a low, menacing voice that chilled her to the bone.

Nonetheless, she lifted her head higher. "Not while there's breath left in my body."

He didn't move at first, as if he couldn't believe the audacity of her statement. Then he chuckled, and the sound of his laughter heated her blood to boiling. How dare he act *amused*, as if he considered her to be a *joke*.

"I told you before, you'll have a position here at the company if you play nice, but you don't know how to play nice, do you?" Albert asked.

"I don't need you to secure a position for me at *my* father's company."

The annoying smirk didn't leave his face. "Do you really think marrying your ex is enough to change your father's mind—convince him you're capable of heading up a company of this size?"

The heat of embarrassment made her cheeks burn. "My marriage to Dante has no bearing on my father's decision."

"Don't play me for a fool!" he snapped in a low voice. "I know exactly what you're doing."

"And what is that?"

"You think by marrying your ex, your father will turn over the company to you when he steps down. After all, Dante Escarra is a very successful man. Why not use his reputation and business acumen to help you grow the company."

He was smarter than she thought. She hoped her plans weren't obvious to anyone else, especially her father.

Annabelle shrugged. "It's true, Daddy admires and respects Dante's abilities as a businessman. He adores him, actually."

Understandably. Dante's rags to riches story had catapulted him to fame and made him the talk of Houston for years. She'd lost track of how many articles she'd seen extolling his brilliance and marveling at his ability to become so wealthy when he started from nothing. He embodied the type of immigrant-American story politicians bragged about while they stumped for office. He was held up as an example of what could happen through sheer grit, determination, and hard work.

"And what about you, Annabelle? Do you adore your ex?"

"Of course. Why do you think I'm going to marry him again?" She held his gaze without blinking.

"Tell me something... How did you convince Dante to marry you again? There must have been something on offer because there's no way he would put up with you when he has women throwing themselves at him at almost every social engagement. At the moment, he's the most eligible man in the city—probably in all of Texas."

"Why do you care?"

"You know why I care," Albert grated between clenched teeth.

"What is this really about, Albert? Did I hurt your feelings when I turned down your tempting offer?" Annabelle asked in a taunting voice.

He'd had the audacity to offer her marriage. She'd almost thrown up.

Albert's nostrils flared as he stared at her. "There's still time to change your mind."

He moved closer, and though her muscles tensed, Annabelle remained in the same pose, hands on her hips.

"Last chance. Marry me, and when the companies merge, we'll be partners in our personal as well as professional lives. Despite your father's reservations, I know you're an intelligent woman. You're smart. Ambitious. We could rule the Houston market together."

His eyes glittered with excitement when all she felt was disgust.

"Gosh, Albert, you sure know how to tempt a girl, but I'd rather jump out of a plane without a parachute into shark-infested waters than marry you and 'rule the Houston market' together. You're about as trustworthy as Satan, which might be an insult to the devil. Listen up and listen good. You will never have my father's company. Ever."

Albert's features tightened with fury, and she waited for one of the outbursts he was known for. Rumor had it, he was a violent control freak whose first wife simply wanted to escape from the marriage and did so with next to nothing.

A smile slid across his face, but that was probably worse. Nothing but calculated evil rested in his expression, and when he looked her up and down, her flesh tingled with distaste, as if a thousand ants ran up and down the length of her arms.

"*You* will never have this company, Annabelle," he said in a soft voice. "I gave you a chance. You could have become my wife, but you chose instead to spit in my face. You'll regret refusing me and regret trying to take this company from under me. Make no mistake about it."

"Go to—"

He grabbed her upper arm in a vise-like grip. "Watch your mouth, little girl. And watch your back."

"You're standing awfully close to my future wife, Albert. Is there something going on that I should know about?"

Dante!

Albert stepped away from her and released a nervous chuckle.

Dante's face was a mask of hard jaws and narrowed eyes. He walked slowly across the carpet, pinning Albert with a steely stare. "You didn't answer my question."

"Of course there isn't anything going on between us. I wanted to express my congratulations to Annabelle since I couldn't attend the engagement party because of a conflict. You're a very lucky man, Dante."

"I know."

"He was about to leave," Annabelle said.

Albert shot her a look. "We'll talk soon."

He left, and Annabelle took a fortifying breath, rubbing her sore arm. Albert had come at her unexpectedly, ready for all-out war.

"What was that about—because I don't believe a word he said."

"It was nothing."

In a numbed state, Annabelle walked to the minibar and fixed a snifter of brandy. She tossed back half the drink, not bothering to savor its fruity notes, and winced as the liquor burned on the way down.

She needed to tread carefully with Albert. He had her father's ear and could quite possibly convince Clifton to move forward as originally planned. Then she'd be out on her ass with the rest of the long-term staff because Albert would never allow her to remain at the company once he took over.

"You're shaking." Dante's eyes zeroed in on the wobbling glass.

Annabelle switched to holding it with both hands. "I'm fine. He—"

"Don't tell me you're fine because it's obvious you're not. What did Albert want? What did he say to you?" The pointed questions were firm and direct, and his eyes never left her face. He paid attention to every movement, analyzing her with his sharp gaze.

She drank the last of her brandy and placed the glass on the counter with a steadier hand. "He—he threatened me."

"*He threatened you?*" Dante repeated in disbelief.

Annabelle nodded and then slowly told him what Albert said.

By the time she finished, Dante's face held a thunderous expression. "He's not getting away with that." He started toward the door.

"Dante, wait!" She grabbed his forearm. "Don't. I've dealt with Albert before."

"He's harassed you before, and you didn't tell me?" he demanded in an elevated voice.

"Before we had our agreement, and I can handle him."

A muscle in his jaw worked. "I'm sure you can, *querida*, but you will soon be my wife. *Handling* Albert is no longer your responsibility." His gaze dropped to her arm and the faint bruise forming there. His eyebrows drew together. "Did he do that?" he asked in a deceptively soft voice.

"I'm asking you not to get involved. Very soon, what Albert did and said won't matter. My father will talk to the board on my behalf. I'm sure of it."

"He could still merge the company with Strong Technology, Inc."

"He won't. Because you're here now."

Something indecipherable flashed in his eyes. "Correct, I am here now."

Dante walked out the door without another word.

As Annabelle watched him leave, two words echoed in her head. *My wife.*

He said the words in a very possessive way. He said the words like he meant them.

The moment in Annabelle's office had caused Dante to forget the reason he went there in the first place. He was in the area and stopped by to tell her that his sister, who had originally thought she wouldn't be able to attend the wedding with the rest of his family, had changed her plans and was now able to come.

He would pass on the information later. Right now, he needed to teach Albert Strong a very important lesson. He couldn't rid his mind of the image of Annabelle shaking. Knowing his proud, independent, strong wife—fiancée, rather—had been bullied by that man infuriated him.

She should never have had to handle him on her own, but now that Dante knew Albert had been harassing her, he would put a stop to it.

He took long, purposeful strides into Strong Technology, Inc. and stopped at the receptionist desk. "Is Albert Strong in?"

The woman at the desk looked up with a practiced smile, which widened with interest when she saw Dante. "Yes, he is. Do you have an appointment, Mr...?"

"No, I don't."

He took off down the hall toward Albert's office. Though he

had never visited the building before, he had done his homework on the way over and knew exactly where Albert's office was located.

The audacity of that man to put his hands on Annabelle. *His* fucking fiancée. Did Albert not know who he was? He was Dante Fucking Escarra. He was weeks away from making vows to protect her and took his role very seriously. No woman of his would have to deal with the likes of Albert while he was fully capable of shielding her from harm.

"Sir, wait!" the young woman called out.

Dante didn't slow down.

An older woman, clearly Albert's executive assistant, tried to intercept him as he neared Albert's office.

"Sir, if you tell me what you need—"

He bulldozed past her and shoved open the door.

"You can't go in there!" she yelled.

Albert was in the middle of pacing, holding a sheet of paper in his hand as if practicing a speech. At the interruption, he stopped his stride across the floor, and a frown creased his forehead. "Dante, what are you—"

Dante grabbed him by the neck and slammed his cheek onto the desk. Behind him, the woman gasped, and Albert expelled a sharp cry as the paper fell from his hand onto the carpet. Dante dragged the older man's left arm behind his back and tightened his fingers around the back of his neck.

Albert whimpered, and his eyes widened with fear. "Wh-what are you doing? What's going on?" he demanded in a trembling voice.

Dante's nostrils flared with a burst of anger, and his body vibrated with fury. He could hire someone to take care of this situation for him, but this was personal. This particular task could not be passed on to anyone else. He relished putting assholes like this in their place and hadn't had the pleasure in a long time.

"Don't you ever put a hand on my fiancée—my future wife—again, ¿*comprendes*?" Dante asked through clenched teeth.

"Yes," Albert squeaked immediately.

"If you come near her again, intimidate her again, in any way —words or actions—I will come back to see you and put my foot so far up your ass, you'll taste leather for months. Do not think I'll send someone else to do my dirty work. I'll do it myself. I *love* dirty work." He bent closer to whisper the next words. "And don't bother calling the police. I learned a long time ago that life is easier with them on my side. They love me at Houston PD, and Chief Charles and I will be playing golf together on Saturday."

With one final shove, Dante straightened. He walked out with the same long strides he used to walk in. Albert's executive assistant hovered outside the door until he had passed, and then she rushed to the aid of her employer.

He heard her whisper, "Are you all right, Mr. Strong?"

He didn't hear the response and didn't need to.

All that mattered was Albert Strong had gotten the message loud and clear.

Unfortunately for him, Dante wasn't done yet.

"**S**hoo," Grace said, adding the universal hand motion at Annabelle.

Dante's family had arrived minutes earlier and after meeting them and making sure everyone was settled out on the terrace, Annabelle hurried into the kitchen. She was nervous. Before their arrival, she changed her hair twice, finally settling on a top knot and small earrings.

"I want to make sure everything is perfect," Annabelle said.

Grace clasped her hands together and directed a motherly look at Annabelle with pursed lips. "Last month I coordinated your engagement party with hundreds of guests. Why do you think I can't handle a simple dinner with seven people?"

The chef, a burly Black man with a bluesy voice, released a hearty chuckle as he arranged the appetizers—crispy empanadas with a Texan twist, stuffed with smoky barbecued meat and accompanied by pineapple salsa. The entire meal was a fusion of Texan and Venezuelan cuisines.

"Give her a break. She's nervous about meeting her future in-laws. She wants to impress them," he said.

"All the more reason why she should go back outside and let us do our job," Grace said pointedly.

She was right, but Chef was also right. Annabelle wanted Dante's family to like her. The first time he and she married, she never met his family, and they divorced so quickly they didn't get a chance to know her. She had no idea what he'd told them about her since then.

"Fine, I'll go, but—"

"No buts." Grace grasped her shoulders and spun her toward the door. "I'll send out the appetizers shortly."

With a gentle push, she forced Annabelle through the open door. Reluctantly, she placed one foot in front of the other and headed toward the terrace, wiping her sweaty hands on her slacks.

The sound of laughter greeted her ears as she approached the gathered group. Everyone was dressed casually for the meeting of the families. Dante's father, Edgar, was in a wheelchair near the pool, chatting with his other son, Emilio, a leaner, younger version of Dante with the same dark hair and dark eyes.

Dante approached, dressed in jeans and a pullover shirt stretched across his broad chest. How did he manage to look sexy in each outfit he wore?

"Everything okay?" he asked in a lowered voice.

"I went to check on the food. Chef and Grace said the meal will be ready on time, and appetizers will arrive in a few minutes."

"Here. You look like you need this." Dante handed her a glass of white wine.

Their fingers touched and sent a spark of awareness along her nerves. The other night she'd dreamt about the kiss at the engagement party and the tingly sensations that had swept through her lady parts in his arms. She woke up with a start, the earthy scent of his cologne so real she became temporarily confused because it was as if he was lying right next to her in the bed.

Annabelle gratefully drank a mouthful of wine. "Do I look nervous?"

"I doubt my family notices, but I know you. I can tell you're... uneasy. Don't worry, I haven't said terrible things about you to my family."

"Even though I deserve it?"

"All they know is our marriage didn't work. I haven't spoken about you in years."

Ouch. That bit of information hit hard and caused a twist of pain in her chest. She didn't want him to badmouth her, but to know she hadn't been mentioned...

"That's good, I guess," Annabelle said, taking another sip of wine.

A member of the staff came out to the terrace and placed small plates and the empanadas on the long, linen-covered table.

Contessa, Dante's mother, stopped talking to Clifton and eyed the food with interest. "Oh, empanadas." Her curly black hair was tapered in the back, and she wore a pair of small diamond-drop earrings that sparkled when the light from the candles in the wrought-iron lanterns hit them.

"The chef created a fusion dinner—a marriage of the cuisine of both cultures—and these empanadas contain barbecued beef," Annabelle explained. "Everyone, please, let's sit, and then you can help yourselves."

Emilio was the first to approach the table, then Marisol, Dante's sister. She had wavy dark-blonde hair and seemed quieter than Emilio. Annabelle sat between her and Dante, while Contessa, Emilio, and Edgar sat on the opposite side. Clifton settled at the head of the table.

The small plates and empanadas were passed around.

"These are delicious," Emilio said, nodding his head as he chewed.

Annabelle stifled a moan. "They are."

Contessa dabbed her mouth with a napkin. "Thank you for inviting us to dinner," she said to Clifton.

"Thank you for joining us. I'm glad we have the opportunity to sit down and meet this time. Our families will be forever joined together because of our children, and it's important we become closer and better acquainted."

Dante's parents nodded and murmured their agreement, while acid-like guilt gnawed at the inside of Annabelle's stomach. Their families were planning for forever, while she and Dante knew about the one-year expiration date on their marriage. She took a swig of water to quell the burn of their lies.

"You have such a beautiful home. Is this one of the houses that you built?" Edgar asked.

Clifton placed another empanada on his plate. "Yes, it is. My company built this house and most of the homes in this development, in fact. My late wife had excellent taste and spent a lot of time decorating this one, though Annie and I have made minor changes in recent years. We've had many events here—family gatherings, dinners like this, and of course the engagement party."

"I wish we could have come to the party. Dante sent photos and a video, and you looked lovely," Contessa said to Annabelle.

She couldn't read Dante's mother. She seemed friendly, but she also knew how mothers and their sons could be, especially someone as accomplished at Dante. His mother would want a special woman for him.

"Thank you."

The same staff member returned, this time accompanied by Grace, and both of them carried platters of food, the mouth-watering aromas mingling with the scent of the magnolias in the yard. They made several trips, each time eliciting *oohs* from the gathered group as they placed the dishes on the table to be served family style.

On the last delivery, Grace stood beside the table. "The chef has prepared a meal to represent Venezuelan cuisine and the best of Texan cuisine. You have tender brisket marinated in his own blend of spices, *arepas*, grilled plantains, and cornbread. Here, there is more grilled meats—sausage and chicken, again with his own blend of spices. Black beans, macaroni and cheese. Please save room for dessert. We have peach cobbler and très leches cake, and I know you don't want to miss either of those."

"So much food. *Ay, Dios*," Clifton said.

The group broke out in laughter, and the tension Annabelle felt—real or imagined—dispersed.

"I did not know you speak Spanish," Edgar said with amusement.

"I don't, but all this food required that exclamation. Thank you, Grace. You, Chef, and Annie did a wonderful job planning the menu. I can't wait to sink my teeth into the brisket and try *arepas* for the first time."

"Only a spoonful of dessert for you," Annabelle reminded him. If she didn't stay on top of his diet, he'd eat himself into a sugar coma. His sweet tooth was legendary.

"I think that requires another *ay, dios*," Emilio remarked.

After another round of laughter, Grace left them alone, and they started passing around the food. When everyone had a full plate, the conversation started in earnest.

"Tell me about the work you do. Dante said you started an app?" Clifton addressed Emilio with his question.

"Yes, it's a rideshare app, *como* Uber and Lyft. They are not available yet in my country, so I created my own. Dante helped me finance the idea. We are a small but growing company, with nine employees."

"Amazing. Congratulations," Clifton said.

"*Gracias*."

Dante looked past Annabelle to his younger sister. "Why are you so quiet tonight?"

"Me?"

"Yes, you."

"I am observing."

"You need to tell them about your accomplishment."

She blushed. "It is not much."

Dante paused after tearing his cornbread in half. "If she won't brag on herself, I'll brag on her. Marisol attends the University of

São Paulo, one of the top schools for veterinary medicine in the world. This is no surprise to our family since she was always bringing home stray animals when she was a child."

They all laughed at the teasing.

"Thanks to Dante, she can go to the university," Contessa said proudly.

"Mama—" Dante started.

"No, I will say this. My son has blessed us all—his family, his community. And now he has blessed us even more with a new daughter." Smiling, she looked directly at Annabelle.

"I'm very lucky we have another chance to be together again," Annabelle said, almost choking on the deceit. Lying to their families was tougher than she expected.

"I must tell you that you are a godsend for my son," Contessa said to Annabelle in a conspiratorial voice, though everyone at the table could hear.

"Mama, *por favor*," Dante said in a hard voice.

She said something in Spanish and waved away his comment. "Why hide the truth? You are together again, and God has answered my prayers. For years, Dante hid his sadness from me, but I know my son. He was not happy. Here, tonight, I see the way he looks at you when you enter the room, and I *know*. This is true love, and he is happy again. He has peace and will have peace for many years to come. Thank you, Annabelle, *mija*. My son is whole once more. I no longer have to worry about him."

She reached across the table and took Annabelle's hand. She didn't know what to say, forcing a smile to her lips as Contessa gave her fingers a grateful squeeze. Shame filled the depths of her soul. The poor woman was imagining things, and the lies she and Dante had perpetrated gave his mother false hope against his imaginary distress.

"Very soon, you will start a family, yes?" Contessa continued.

Annabelle stiffened.

"*Contessa*, you will embarrass her," Edgar said.

"I only ask the question. I do not embarrass you, Annabelle?" Contessa asked in the most innocent voice.

"We do eventually want to start a family, but we cannot rush," Dante interrupted smoothly. "All in due time, Mama."

"I am an old woman. I will not live forever." Contessa stuck her fork in a plantain.

"I have to interject here and say I also look forward to the day when I will have grandchildren. I'll be retiring soon, so the timing is perfect," Clifton said with a hopeful glint in his eyes.

Oh for goodness' sake! Not her father too.

Cutting the tender brisket with a knife, Annabelle kept her eyes trained on her plate.

Babies had been the furthest thing from her mind, but this conversation made her wonder...

If she and Dante had a son, what would he look like? Would he have dimples like his father? She imagined chasing a pint-sized version of Dante around the yard, teaching him to swim, showering him with kisses as she tucked him in at night. She would love to have a little girl too. The kids would learn Spanish, of course, and spend summers in Venezuela visiting their *abuelos* to learn about their Latin heritage.

Annabelle blinked, shocked at the direction of her thoughts. What was she thinking? A future together with children was never going to happen.

"Ah, you see, I am not the only person who wishes for grand-children," Contessa said to her husband. She turned to Clifton. "We will pray for a long and happy marriage and healthy babies."

"Amen," Clifton said.

Thankfully, the topic of conversation shifted, and the Escarras shared details of their life in Venezuela and how much they enjoyed traveling to the United States. They had visited several times over the years—not only Texas but California and New York. Contessa insisted Clifton and Annabelle must come to their home in Venezuela, so they could return the hospitality they received.

Other than the moment of discomfort Annabelle experienced when they talked about grandchildren, the conversation flowed smoothly as the families shared stories and laughter. She learned more details about Dante's delinquent behavior—details he hadn't shared with her. Then her father thoroughly embarrassed her by informing their guests about *her* behavior and how pleased he was to see her mature from a partying socialite to the woman she had become.

The night ended with the sweet desserts, and everyone agreed the cake and cobbler were a fitting finish to an excellent meal.

At the end of the evening, the group slowly made their way to the door. In the foyer, Contessa paused and looked expectantly between Dante and Annabelle. "You are coming with us?" she asked.

Dante was going to take his family to a hotel before going home. Despite his repeated requests, they insisted on staying at a hotel, so he booked two suites at the best hotel in Houston—one for his sister and brother to share and the other for his parents. According to Contessa, they didn't want to intrude because he and Annabelle would be married at the end of the week and would need their privacy.

"No, I'm staying at home until our wedding night," Annabelle answered.

She wasn't moving in any of her belongings, either. Dante thought her reservations were ridiculous, calling them a 'silly notion of impropriety,' especially since they had been married before, but she didn't want to move in with him until they were legally married again.

It was for the best since she couldn't erase the kiss from her mind, and she had been very aware of Dante all night. Every time his knee bumped hers or his hand brushed hers, her heart raced annoyingly fast. Every so often the phantom taste of him surfaced in her mouth, and more than once, she'd caught herself scrolling the tip of her tongue against her teeth in an effort to relive his flavor.

"Good night, *querida*."

As Dante bent to give her a kiss, her stomach tightened. His lips barely brushed her cheek but sent her heart racing again.

"Good night," Annabelle said.

She and her father stepped outside and watched the Escarras drive away before returning inside and closing the door.

14

Today was his wedding day, for the second time.

Dante stood in front of the mirror in a black tux. The stylist he had hired for the occasion had already left, and he was alone with his brother, Emilio, and Sebastian inside the groom suite of the venue. The 12-acre property included a chapel, a grand reception hall, and a rural landscape with rolling pastures and a pond.

"How do you feel?" Emilio asked from the sofa.

"Excellent," Dante answered. It was not an exaggeration. He was oddly energized and upbeat.

"That makes one of us," Sebastian muttered, pouring himself a glass of water.

Dante glanced at him through the mirror. "You worry too much."

"One of us has to. You're going to give me an ulcer one of these days with the shit you pull."

Dante brushed a loose thread from his shoulder. "Don't blame me if you have an ulcer."

"What shit are you pulling?" Emilio asked with a frown.

Sebastian and Dante exchanged a look. Dante hadn't told

anyone in his family that his marriage to Annabelle was simply a ruse for them to accomplish their personal goals.

Sebastian smiled at Dante's brother. "I meant that I can't believe he's getting married to the same woman again. Hopefully, things will work out better this time around."

"She seems nice to me. She was friendly at dinner. I do wonder why she is marrying my brother."

He smirked while Sebastian snorted a brief laugh.

Dante shot his brother a dark scowl. "*Que ladilla t'eres.*"

Emilio laughed. "I am not being annoying. I am really surprised."

Dante turned away from the mirror. "I better go to the chapel before I strangle you," he said.

"Before we leave, I want to make a toast." The words rushed from Emilio's mouth.

The venue had provided a table filled with snacks, bottled water, and chilled champagne. His brother handed out the glasses and then opened the champagne with a loud pop. He poured them each a glass of the sparkling wine and took a deep breath.

"I know I have made some jokes, but I believe you and Annabelle will have a successful marriage this time. She is good for you, I believe. She is no—as they say in English—push over."

"No, she is not," Dante conceded.

"And I know you have not told us half of what you went through when you moved to this country. Thank you for all you have done, Dante. I wish you and Annabelle many years of happiness together. You deserve it."

The moment became charged with emotion. Dante had achieved his objectives in the United States, and the disrespect and struggles he went through as a teen and young man were worth the sacrifice to see his family thrive.

He gripped his younger brother's shoulder and pulled him into a one-armed hug. Kissing his temple, he whispered, "*Te amo, hermanito.*"

Emilio squeezed him back. When he pulled away, he ducked his head and wiped a finger across his eye. He then looked expectantly at Sebastian, who squared his shoulders and cleared his throat.

"I, er, I don't have much to say, except I'm honored to stand beside you again, and I wish you the best. I hope you get everything you want out of this marriage," he said with a meaningful look.

The three men touched their glasses together and then tipped them to their lips. A few minutes later, they left the groom's suite.

When Dante and Annabelle married the first time, Clifton hadn't spared any expense giving his daughter a lavish ceremony. This time was no less grand, but the guest list was much shorter. The engagement party had included over two hundred people, but there were fewer than one hundred people in attendance today. The smaller, more intimate gathering consisted of mostly family and friends.

Dante went to stand at the front of the chapel and spotted the rest of his family in the front row. His sister smiled, and he smiled back. Beside her, his mother was the picture of effortless grace, her hands folded in her lap. She glanced briefly at him, her face full of pride and excitement about his future and those grandchildren she'd hinted about when both families ate dinner together.

Guilt ate at him, something he seldom allowed himself to feel. Deceiving family was different from getting over on business rivals. He hated lying to his parents and siblings and didn't look forward to having to tell them in a year that he and Annabelle had split again. But he'd have the one object he wanted more than anything in the world. The Hilderbrandt Plaza. The discomfort, the guilt, and the resulting conversations with his family a year from now would all be worth it to have the iconic building in his portfolio.

It would prove the poor kid from Venezuela had arrived. He

had succeeded when others doubted. Anticipation thrummed in his veins for the moment when he achieved his goal.

Soft music piped in through speakers signaled the beginning of the ceremony. The daughters of Annabelle's cousin on her father's side came down the aisle, adorable little blondes in powder-blue dresses with gold sashes. They dropped the flowers onto the white runner to the *oohs* and *ahhs* of the guests. Then the ring bearer came down the aisle dressed in a suit, his brown face smiling bashfully before taking his place in the audience.

There was a lull before Sebastian and Emilio escorted Lacey and another of Annabelle's friends down the aisle. Each of them took their place on the dais along with Dante and the priest.

The double doors closed for several minutes and then opened again. Music filled the air, and Dante lifted his gaze to the back of the church. Annabelle and her father appeared and started the march down the aisle. Some of the guests stood to watch their progression, while others whispered furiously to each other. There were no phones allowed, which meant only the videographer and photographer captured the moment.

"Damn," Sebastian murmured beside him.

Damn indeed. Dante held his breath. Annabelle was a vision in a pearl-white dress.

Like déjà vu, he watched her come toward him, a stunning bride on her father's arm. Over the course of their short-lived relationship, he'd called her several things—*mi amor, mi princesa, querida*, but no endearment fit her better than *mi reina*. Queen was the most apt description for a woman who moved with the grace of royalty. That was Annabelle every day and certainly today.

His stomach contracted, but not in fear or dread. No, this was something else altogether. Excitement. Fervent anticipation. He looked forward to their union in a way he hadn't expected— all because of the vision coming toward him in a dress with an off-the-shoulder lace top and see through sleeves. The floral pattern and beadwork made the dress shimmer and shine. The long, elaborate train floated behind her as she herself seemed to float beside her father down the aisle.

"Who presents this woman to be joined with this man?" the priest asked.

"I do, her father," Clifton said. He kissed his daughter's cheek and then placed her hand in Dante's.

Annabelle then joined Dante on the dais, and the ceremony began with a prayer.

When they first married, Dante and Annabelle had read unique vows to each other. Not this time. Because this time wasn't real. They both had an ulterior motive for entering into this marriage.

One year. Then it would be over. At this moment, he wasn't sure that's what he wanted.

The conversation about grandchildren earlier in the week came back to him, and he suddenly imagined himself and Annabelle with a family. Three or four little ones—a thought he had never experienced with any other woman. It seemed right that, if he did have children, she should be their mother.

What if...?

A surge of regret filled him, and a heavy weight spread throughout his chest cavity.

Eyes locked on Annabelle, he repeated the words as instructed, and when the officiant asked for the rings, Dante took Annabelle's hand in his. Her fingers slightly trembled as he slipped the ring on her finger. Did she feel it too? The oppressive weight of what they were doing? Could this mockery of a marriage become more?

An indescribable emotion clogged his throat. She was going to be his wife again. *His* wife. No one else's.

They locked eyes as he repeated the words, "With this ring, I take you as my spouse and commit to being your partner in life. I promise to forsake all others, protect you, and care for you."

The rest of the ceremony took place in a vacuum. Dante barely heard what the priest said or the words that Annabelle repeated. All he could think was how they were binding themselves to each other. In front of family, friends, and God.

"You may kiss the bride."

They both knew this moment was coming, yet they looked at each other for a beat. Then the longing to experience the softness of her mouth again overtook him. Dante moved first, stepping closer and kissing Annabelle on the lips. The kiss should have been brief. There was absolutely no reason to prolong it, but her lips were soft and malleable, sending a burst of desire through him like the night of their engagement party.

A soft sigh escaped from her, and he groaned as he angled his head and kissed her deeper, plucking her lower between his teeth while one hand went to the back of her neck to apply pressure.

She was exquisite and tasted like perfection. Like perfectly ripe fruit—succulent and juicy and delicious. He could kiss her forever and almost did. The throb of desire unfurled in his loins, and only upon hearing the snickers of their guests did he remember they were the center of attention in a public place.

Finally, they withdrew from each other. Or rather, he released her—reluctantly. His breathing was labored, and a deep hunger filled him as he watched her bright eyes and flushed cheeks. No, more than hunger. Craving. Craving to bury himself inside her as deep as he could possibly go.

"May this union bring you joy, love, and fulfillment throughout your journey together," the priest said.

Dante's heart thudded in his chest at the chaotic thoughts swirling through his head. Years ago, she had slipped through his fingers, and he'd lost his friend, his lover, his future. They had been good together when they weren't miserable.

Could they take this opportunity to fix the mistakes of the past?

15

It was over. Finally.

The wedding. The reception. Annabelle had forgotten how exhausting being a bride could be. Maybe because last time she'd been happy. This time, the smiling and pretending took more energy than she could have ever imagined. Beside her in the back of a limousine with *Just Married* framed by flowers and attached to the back, Dante sat with the top button on his shirt undone and his tie missing. No telling where that was. He'd gotten rid of the neckwear immediately after their first dance at the reception.

The kiss at the end of the ceremony took place in front of the church hours before, but her mouth continued to sing from the pressure of his. The kiss had been a stamp. A declaration of ownership. Every time her eyes found Dante's at the reception, her pulse raced anew, as if in anticipation of the night ahead.

They had ridden from the venue in silence, leaving behind cheering guests who yelled best wishes at them as they embarked on their new life together. Hah. If only they knew the truth. This marriage was a farce. A means to an end for both of them.

The limousine cruised to a stop, and the driver opened the door and helped her from the car.

"Thank you," Annabelle said.

She wore the same dress from the ceremony but had removed the detachable train for the reception.

She gazed up at the large, textured exterior of the two-story structure made of sand-colored stucco that would be her home for the next year. Much different from the home she and Dante moved into the first time they married. At the time, her father had gifted them an apartment in one of his buildings, which Dante had begrudgingly accepted.

This place, however, was located in River Oaks behind a gate, an exquisite example of Mediterranean architecture, enclosed by a high wood fence and with a boundary of trees for additional privacy. She looked forward to exploring the property, which she knew included a private tennis court, a four-car garage, an elevator, and an outdoor kitchen and living space overlooking the swimming pool.

Annabelle gathered her skirt and walked toward the door. Halfway there, her feet were swept out from under her, and she let out a soft gasp as Dante lifted her into his strong arms.

"What are you doing?" she asked.

He looked at her with his trademark smirk. "This is tradition," he explained.

"Put me down," she whispered, so the driver who had hurried ahead of them to open the door to the house couldn't hear.

"Once we have crossed the threshold," Dante replied in a calm voice.

Reluctantly, she looped her arms around his neck, nestling her body against his and inhaling the inviting musk of his earthy cologne. He carried her into an elegant foyer designed in black and white. Her mouth fell open at the sight of the sparkling floors covered in ivory marble tile and the crystal chandelier hanging from the two-story ceiling.

Directly across from the double staircase with black handrails, an entry table stood in the middle with a midnight vase holding a gorgeous bouquet of flowers. To the left, three archways led the way into a small dining room and to the right, another three archways led to a sitting room with a television mounted above the fireplace.

This house was smaller than the one she'd grown up in but certainly grander and more spacious than the apartment they lived in before. The furnishings and architectural details demonstrated wealth while keeping the decor tasteful. The young man from Venezuela had come a long way.

"Beautiful," Annabelle breathed.

"You sound surprised," Dante said.

"Not really, but your designer did an excellent job."

"I agree. Welcome to your new home." He placed her on her feet.

"Thank you."

Annabelle gathered her skirt, and they climbed the stairs to the second floor. Dante led her to the master bedroom located behind walnut double doors with carvings etched into the wood.

"Gorgeous and such detail," she whispered, running her fingers over a beach scene with waves crashing into the shore.

"I had the doors imported from Brazil." Dante pushed them open.

Inside, the bedroom had a much more calming atmosphere than the sparkle of the grand foyer downstairs. The decor consisted of Earth tones with splashes of deep blue and forest green dominating. In the middle of the room with the headboard pushed against the wall was an enormous bed, the size of two kings. On either side were mahogany tables, and one of them had several hard cover titles stacked on top of it.

A separate sitting room contained a fireplace and comfortable looking chairs and tables for relaxing, and double doors led to the balcony beyond.

"This is my room. Yours is this way."

Dante led her into the hall to the other room, smaller and more modestly furnished, but no less appealing in design. A canopied bed was covered in white linens, with a small area containing two armchairs on opposite sides of a coffee table. The furniture rested in front of a bay window overlooking the lit tennis court below. The colors made the room bright and airy, in contrast to the warmth and cozy atmosphere of the master bedroom.

"Most of your belongings have been unpacked," he said, indicating her vanity against one wall with an inclination of his head.

He swung open a door which led to a large dressing room. "Your clothes are in here."

She checked, and sure enough, her clothes had been unpacked and hung on hangers, though with a quick glance she knew she'd have to do a little bit of rearranging.

She felt Dante's eyes on her and turned to see him in a relaxed position, one shoulder resting against the door jamb as he watched her with an inscrutable expression in his eyes.

What was he thinking?

Her chest tightened with nerves. He'd adhered to her request that they sleep in separate rooms, yet somehow she found herself having to brush aside disappointment.

"So, Señora Escarra, is everything to your liking?" he asked in a lazy tone.

Annabelle had no plans to change her name, but Mrs. Escarra had a nice ring to it. Annabelle Escarra. Annabelle Buchanan-Escarra.

She became annoyed with herself. She shouldn't have such thoughts.

"Yes, everything is fine," she answered, walking past him into the bedroom.

"*Bueno.* It's been a long day, and I think it's time for bed, don't you? I will leave you alone. Sweet dreams, *mi bella esposa.*"

With those words, Dante walked away and closed the door on the way out.

ANNABELLE TOOK HER TIME WASHING HER FACE AND APPLYING eye cream and moisturizer. She removed the clips from her hair and then brushed the strands smooth before braiding them into a plait which hung down the middle of her back.

Though she'd been clear they would not be having sex in this marriage, tonight was their wedding night. Sleeping in separate rooms seemed odd and out of place, a far cry from their first wedding night when they barely made it to the bed because they'd started making love as Dante carried her over the threshold. They fell onto the bed together, and he gazed down into her eyes, his bright and lively in a way she had never seen before. She'd been convinced right then that his love was true and would last forever.

"We are home, Señora Escarra."

"Yes, we are, Señor Escarra. You and me, together forever."

"Forever. Nothing will ever tear us apart."

They had lied to each other. Six months later, the cracks started. Narrow tears in the fabric of their marriage eventually tore them apart at the seams.

Sometimes she wished she could forget how good their life used to be, but maybe the reminders were for the best. She needed those memories to remind her that she would never have the same type of happiness again. At least, not with Dante.

Her father had offered Dante a position at Buchanan & Buchanan when they married, but he insisted on working two jobs while juggling his real estate aspirations on the side.

"I don't want a handout," Dante said, sounding aggravated as he packed his lunch for a long workday. He had bought another property, and he and Sebastian were fixing it up themselves to save money.

"He's not giving you a handout. He's trying to be helpful," Annabelle insisted.

Dante slammed a hand on the kitchen counter, and she jumped.

"He has done enough. This apartment, the furniture, everything. He has been very generous. I could never afford all of this on my own. The money I save, I can invest into another property. And then another."

She swallowed the pain of disappointment. She wished he wasn't so obsessed with properties and spreadsheets and toiling and laboring every single day. They were newlyweds, and she wanted to enjoy their married life more. Instead, he was gone most of the time.

"You're working too hard."

"No!" The sharpness in his tone surprised her. "I work hard, but not too hard. I do this because it will help me achieve my goals. Be patient, querida. You will see, the sacrifices will all be worth it."

Padding into the bedroom, Annabelle walked to the window overlooking the illuminated tennis court. Beyond the court was a curtain of trees and a privacy fence separating their property from the next one.

Their property.

She shouldn't think in those terms. This was Dante's house.

She turned out the light and climbed into bed. Lying on the soft mattress, she stared up at the canopy, wondering if Dante was asleep yet.

Their marriage had nothing to do with love and happily ever after this time. She needed to focus on the prize, which was convincing her father to install her as the next CEO.

Nothing else mattered.

❧ 16 ❧

"**G**ood morning," Annabelle said as she walked into the dining room.

Dante was already there eating breakfast, an iPad beside his plate.

She hadn't seen much of him this weekend. The day after their wedding, he went to play golf, as if he didn't have a new wife. She didn't know what she'd expected, but she hadn't expected to be thoroughly ignored.

They ate dinner together and then went their separate ways afterward—Dante going to his home office to work, and Annabelle focused on reorganizing her clothes and other items. The next day, they met his family for breakfast. After the meal, she said goodbye and went to work, but Dante had taken the morning off and took them to the airport. Last night, he told her they had arrived safely in Venezuela.

"Good morning," he murmured. He never looked up from the iPad.

She purposely bumped the table when she sat down, which got his attention. He looked up with a frown.

"Excuse me," Annabelle said sweetly.

Dante dabbed his mouth with a cloth napkin. Resting his

forearm on the edge of the table, he watched her with his dark, piercing gaze. "Did you sleep well last night?"

"I did. And the night before," Annabelle replied.

"Good, I'm glad to hear you're comfortable. I have to fly to Las Vegas today. I'll be gone the rest of the week."

What? The announcement startled her. *We just got married!* she wanted to scream. Instead, she nodded and smiled. "Great. I'll have the place all to myself."

"Try not to break anything," he said dryly.

"I won't do my best," she said in a saccharine-filled voice.

Instead of replying, Dante shook his head and nudged aside his plate.

"I have some news." Annabelle poured orange juice in her glass.

A female member of the staff entered with a plate of food for her—eggs over easy, sausage, and biscuits. On the way out the dining room, she picked up Dante's dish.

Annabelle began spreading butter on her bread. "The invitation to Nolson Hilderbrandt's annual party arrived. Mine was sent to my father's address. The party is in three weeks."

Dante's eyes gleamed with interest. "Excellent."

Interesting. She had the distinct impression he was tamping down his excitement.

"I'll RSVP for the two of us. This year there's a casino night theme. There isn't usually a theme, but it should be fun. His wife, Khuyen, came up with the idea."

"I'm looking forward to it." Dante lifted his cup of coffee to his lips. The movement pushed his big biceps into prominence beneath the white dress shirt.

Yesterday, Annabelle had seen him in his home gym wearing a gray crew neck tank and black shorts. A thin film of sweat made his skin glisten as his large fists pummeled the punching bag. His muscles contracted and loosened with each blow, and her entire body stilled as she watched him.

Dante believed mental health was tied to physical health.

When they were married before, he did muscle training on Mondays, Wednesdays, and Fridays. Tuesdays, Thursdays, and Saturdays were for cardio. On Sundays he "worked out" mentally by reading for hours. He read during the week, too, but only here and there. On Sundays, he spent hours reading.

It seemed he maintained the same routine, which came as no surprise. He was a man of discipline.

Dante pushed back his chair and stood, towering over the table. "I'll go straight from work to the airport. I'll see you this weekend."

He didn't wait for her to respond and left her alone in the dining room.

Slowly, Annabelle placed her fork on the plate. She did a good job of pretending indifference around him, but emotion sat in her chest like a pile of bricks, and she had the sudden urge to cry. Only a few days after her wedding, Dante was leaving her alone in the house to go off to Las Vegas.

Pushing back her chair, she rose from the table too. Viviana, the housekeeper, came in and frowned at her full plate. Viviana was from Venezuela and one of several full-time staff who worked for Dante.

"You are not satisfied with the meal, *señora?*"

"The meal was delicious, but I wasn't very hungry. I'll see you after work. I guess you know I'll be dining alone this evening?"

"Yes, *señora.*"

"Anything you want to prepare for dinner will be fine."

"Are you sure? You are not in the mood for anything special?"

"No."

"I will make something special for you."

Her eyes filled with sympathy, and Annabelle avoided her gaze. She didn't want pity. So what if her husband didn't want to spend time with her and would rather run off to conduct business in Las Vegas? She'd be fine. Soon—very soon—she'd have the one thing she wanted most. Control of her father's business and his respect when she did a good job.

Nothing else matters, she reminded herself.

"Thank you." Annabelle hurried from the dining room.

She drove to the office, and when she arrived went to work right away reviewing renovation plans for an apartment complex they had recently purchased. The buildings needed a lot of work, and renovations were sometimes problematic because of hidden defects which could delay progress or increase costs.

The phone on her desk rang, and she absentmindedly picked it up. "Hello?"

"Annie, I have something important to discuss with you. Would you come into my office for a moment?" her father asked.

She perked up, her attention leaving the paperwork in front of her. "Sure. I'll be right there."

After hanging up, Annabelle sat without moving and contemplated what her father could possibly want. It was unusual for him to call her into his office. He usually worked closely with the COO and left her to her own devices as chief development officer.

Was this the moment she had been waiting for? Was this when he told her that he wanted her to take over the company? Only a few days had passed since the wedding. It was too soon, surely, yet she couldn't help but hope.

Standing, she straightened her skirt, as if she was going in for an interview and needed to look her best. She left her office and walked down the hall toward her father's office. Nervous flutters filled her belly, but she offered friendly smiles to staff she passed along the way.

At the door, she gently knocked and then let herself inside. Clifton faced the window, hands crossed behind his back. When she entered, he turned, and his bearded face broke into a smile.

"Come in and have a seat."

Annabelle did as he asked, lowering into one of the guest chairs.

He moved to stand behind the desk. "How are the renovations on the Pine Forest property?" he asked.

"Nothing out of the ordinary so far. The contractors should have phase one of the renovations complete in a few weeks."

"What about the Angel Head condominium conversion?"

"We hit a snag with the water department, but Julie's going down there in the morning to get the situation cleared up. I told her she was not allowed to leave without an approval, so we could begin installing the meters for each unit."

"Good, good," her father said, nodding his head. Eyes trained on the desk below him, he frowned, as if thinking about what to say next.

Annabelle waited patiently for him to speak.

Finally, he lifted his gaze. "I called you in here because the past couple of months I've struggled with a decision. My retirement is coming up, and I've been thinking about the company and what I want for Buchanan & Buchanan after I leave."

Annabelle remained silent, holding her breath, nails digging into the clenched palms resting on either side of her thighs.

"When Cliffy passed, I wasn't sure what would become of Buchanan & Buchanan because I had always envisioned him taking over one day, the way the men in my family have since the founding of the company. All this..." He spread his arms to encompass the room. "Was supposed to be his domain."

Heart heavy, Annabelle didn't move, anxiously awaiting his next words.

"Some years ago, I decided merging the company with Strong Technology, Inc. was the right decision. I know what you think of Albert, but he and I go way back, and he's in a complementary business. I strongly believe having him take charge of B&B could lead the company into a new era."

Oh no. Was he going to break her heart?

"Daddy—"

Clifton lifted his hand. "Let me finish. Real estate is a cutthroat business, as you know, and running *this* company is not easy. For a very long time, I believed the role of CEO was not the right one for a woman—certainly not my daughter. The demands of heading a company is not what I wanted for you, but watching you the past few years has made me rethink my stance. You're fair and intelligent and don't make rash decisions. You're a good leader and respected by the staff. Therefore, I've had a change of heart."

Annabelle breathed easier, the heaviness in her chest lifting.

He continued. "Although I believe Albert would make a great CEO of the merged companies, I also believe you would do a great job if given the chance to take the reins of B&B. So I called you in here to tell you my decision. If you're interested, I would like you to become the new CEO of Buchanan & Buchanan."

Inside, Annabelle screamed *Hallelujah!*, but she remained calm on the outside. "Yes, I'm very interested."

For the first time, a smile touched the corners of her father's mouth. "Marrying Dante should prove beneficial to you. I feel better knowing if problems arise you have a man beside you who could help you sort through issues. He has a great mind, and with him consulting, you could build B&B into the company I didn't. You could surpass my expectations."

Annabelle blew out a shocked breath. This was the moment she had been waiting for, and now that it had arrived, she was overwhelmed. Elated, but overwhelmed.

"Thank you. I promise I won't let you down."

His face softened. "I know you won't, honey. I'm confident you'll do well. The board has its next quarterly meeting next month, and I'll make my recommendation then."

Annabelle jumped up from her seat and rushed around to the other side of the desk. She flung her arms around her father's neck, and he chuckled, wrapping his arms around her too.

"Thank you," she said again, voice muffled against his chest. "I have lots of ideas, and I'm going to work so hard." He'd only given her a shot because he believed if she ran into problems, Dante could guide her out of them, but at least he'd given her a shot.

Clifton patted her back. "I can't wait to see what you do."

A nnabelle's arms sliced through the warm water. Dante's pool was larger than the one at her father's home, and she appreciated the extra workout. By the time she reached the end, she sensed she wasn't alone. With a quick glance over her shoulder, she saw Dante watching her with one hand tucked into his pants pocket.

Taking a deep breath, she pushed off below the water and surfaced with strong kicks and arm strokes. Arriving at Dante's end of the pool, she climbed the stairs out of the water, conscious of the string bikini barely containing her breasts and barely covering her privates. Pinpricks of heat scraped her skin as his gaze followed her walk across the concrete.

"You have a tattoo," he murmured.

A colorful butterfly was inked into her hip. She'd gotten the design on impulse, months after her divorce from Dante when she decided to go to college. It was a symbol of her rebirth after she'd grieved the demise of her marriage. In her mind, she had been transformed, leaving the cocoon of being a daughter, then a wife, finally experiencing the freedom to learn who she really was and start a new life.

"I've had it for years." Annabelle lifted a fluffy towel from one of the chairs and wrapped it around her body. She squeezed excess water from her hair and then sat down at the table. Picking up a few nuts from the platter of finger food Viviana had brought out for her, she popped them into her mouth.

"When did you get it?" he asked.

"Six months after we divorced." She gazed up at him but couldn't see his expression. With his back to the light and the glittering pool water, his face was cast in shadow. "Your text said you'd be back sooner. You missed dinner."

"I stopped by the office when I landed."

Of course he did. "Some things never change. How was your trip?"

There was a brief silence before he answered. Probably because of her snide remark. "Successful. I signed a deal to become one of several investors in a casino on the strip."

Her eyebrows lifted higher. "Wow. Congratulations."

"Thank you. It's a deal I've been working on for a while."

"I have good news too. While you were gone, my father offered me the CEO position."

"Anna, that's wonderful." His voice held genuine happiness for her.

"Thanks." Annabelle ate a peanut. "The past few days, I've been thinking about Albert. I haven't heard from him since you saw him in my office. You went to see him, didn't you?"

"Yes."

He didn't hesitate. No surprise. Dante never hid the truth. He spoke bluntly and truthfully, direct and cutting if necessary.

"After I asked you not to."

"I told you why that was impossible." He strolled over to the table and popped a cube of cheese in his mouth. Closer now, she saw his face clearly.

"Because I'm your wife. Yet you planned a business trip without telling me." She failed at keeping the bitterness from her voice.

He studied her in silence, and she pretended not to notice, keeping her gaze on the rippling pool water.

"I... should not have left so abruptly. I should have told you about my plans earlier, and I should have kept in touch while I was gone."

Wait a minute, had *Dante* just apologized? Well, not apologized exactly, but certainly admitted he was wrong. Annabelle didn't know what to say.

"You're a busy man."

His eyes bored into her. "That's no excuse."

She shrugged, though her heart ached for... something. "This isn't a real marriage."

"Why do you feel the need to remind me?"

She wasn't reminding him. She was reminding herself. She hated the awkwardness between them and despised her internal longing for a connection to someone—to *him*. They used to be close and shared everything. Told each other their secrets and dreams. They were playful. Comparing their marriage before and their marriage now... Well, there was no comparison, and in a short time, the difference already felt like torture.

"I never want to leave here," Annabelle said, floating on top of the waves. She sighed happily.

They'd driven down to Galveston for the weekend to take a look at a vacation rental that Dante was interested in purchasing. He decided not to buy the property, but they took advantage of the idyllic location and spent hours deep-sea fishing and racing each other on jet skis. Last night, they dined at a restaurant with some of the best seafood she'd ever tasted. She could still taste the buttery, tender fish.

"One day, I will own a place here, on the water." Dante stood with the sea water halfway up to his chest, a faraway look in his eyes.

Annabelle wrapped her arms and legs around him, and his hands cupped her bottom.

"You'll do it, too. I know you will. This one didn't work out, but there will be others." Her thumb stroked his cheek, forcing a smile to his face and chasing away the frown from his brow.

He squeezed her bottom, and she moaned softly. She kissed his neck.

"Behave, querida. We're in public."

"You started it." She plucked at his skin with her teeth.

"Time to go," Dante said, starting toward the shore.

Annabelle giggled and whispered dirty words about what she wanted to do to him in his ear, which made him walk faster.

"I don't feel the need to remind you. It's just... Never mind." Annabelle shook her head. "Viviana left dinner for you in the warmer."

"I already ate. Congratulations on becoming the CEO. I know you'll do an excellent job. Cliffy would be proud."

Her breath caught at the mention of her brother and tears misted her eyes, but she quickly blinked them away. "I hope so."

"Good night, Anna."

"Good night."

She didn't watch him walk away but heard the opening and closing of the door. Sighing, she gazed up at the black sky. Why did she think marrying him and moving in together was a good idea? It had been an impulsive, desperate decision and not clearly thought through.

She had counted on anger and acrimony to get her through the 365 days, but another emotion was creeping in, and she was afraid to analyze what the emotion was and what it meant.

Pushing up from the chair, Annabelle took the platter of snacks inside and then climbed the stairs to the second floor. The house was quiet. Passing by Dante's bedroom, she couldn't tell if he was awake or not. If he was, he was probably reading before he went to sleep.

She should stop worrying about him and thinking about him. He didn't think about *her*. He went to Las Vegas and closed a lucrative deal and probably hadn't thought of her once while there. In fact, he clearly hadn't because only after she made a snide remark about his departure did he express remorse for his rude behavior.

In her bedroom, Annabelle took a quick shower and washed

and blow-dried her hair. She combed through her leave-in conditioner and then braided her hair into one long plait. By the time she finished, her eyes were drooping.

She plodded toward the bed, but something on her vanity caught the corner of her eye. Slowly, she approached, her frown of confusion deepening. There was a new vintage perfume bottle on the table, with a card propped against it. She opened the envelope and read the message.

I saw this in Las Vegas and thought you might want to add it to your collection.

She inhaled a sharp breath. No way did Dante happen to run across a vintage perfume bottle. He had to go looking for it. Occasionally, she visited a perfume bottle dealer, but that wasn't her favorite way to find pieces. She found them at antique shops, vintage stores, and estate sales. The hunt was part of the fun of collecting them.

She held up the bottle, which contained a few drops of perfume. The container was gorgeous, made of crystal on a legged pedestal with a gold stopper that had a floral dogwood design. The bottle easily cost over a hundred dollars. She lifted it to her nose and inhaled the bouquet.

Biting her bottom lip, she gazed down at Dante's note, written in his large scrawl.

He *had* thought of her. Something inside her shifted. She placed the note in one of the drawers and replaced the bottle on the table.

Sitting on the edge of the bed, she thought about what this meant. Did he care for her more than he let on? She didn't know, and not knowing was driving her crazy. She needed answers.

Annabelle hopped up from the bed and headed to Dante's room. She knocked on the door, which served to infuriate her—because why was she knocking on her husband's door?

"Come in."

With a barrage of nervous flutters filling her stomach, she took a deep breath and pushed her way inside. Dante was standing near the sitting room in his slacks from earlier, but his chest was bare. She gulped, her heart hammering like a fist against her ribs. His magnificent body was made up of sinewy muscle, his chest and forearms sprinkled with hair.

A painful ache blossomed in her core as the dark need of desire snaked through her. That pissed her off. These feelings plaguing her day after day were his fault.

"I saw the perfume bottle you brought me. Why did you do that?"

One eyebrow winged upward. "A simple thank you would be enough."

She blushed. "Thank you, but I need my question answered. You're sending conflicting messages. You ignore me, but then you bring back a vintage perfume bottle because you know I collect them. You treat me with indifference, but you're constantly touching me and... and kissing me. You're trying to seduce me, and it won't work."

"No?"

"No. Do you know why?"

"Tell me." He looked amused.

"Because this isn't real."

"You're lying to yourself, *querida*. Our marriage might not last, but it's real. And this"—he gestured between them—"what we feel when we're near each other, is *very* real."

❦ 18 ❦

S he was in denial. Clearly, by the way her face shuttered, but what was the point of lying when they could be giving each other pleasure instead?

"We need each other in more ways than one," Dante said.

The bikini she had worn earlier was tempting, and he'd barely been able to peel his eyes from her. When she came out of the water, her drenched body had been exquisite to behold. With water droplets glimmering like diamonds on her hair and skin, he'd almost tossed her over his shoulder and taken her upstairs right then.

The pajamas she wore now were equally tempting. A pair of pale-green shorts showed off her glorious golden-brown legs and a matching top with spaghetti straps draped over her full, unfettered breasts and made him long to cup them in his hands. Her hard nipples pressed against the thin fabric, exposing the truth she preferred to hide—that she wanted him.

"We are married for one reason and one reason only. I want to head up Buchanan & Buchanan, and you want the Hilderbrandt building. There is no other reason," Annabelle said.

"Then why do you care if I spend time with you or pay attention to you?"

She didn't have an answer, but he knew why. Time to give Annabelle an education about herself.

"Because you want it all, don't you? It's not enough that we're married. You want me wrapped around your finger."

She shook her head. "Not true."

"Oh, but it is. You want me wrapped around your finger so you can control me like you did before."

"I controlled you?" she said in a raised voice. "That's a laugh. Six months into our marriage, you practically disappeared. I hardly saw you, which I guess I should be used to because we're basically reliving the past, aren't we?"

"I was working, trying to build something from scratch."

"You didn't have to start from scratch. My father offered you a job, and you refused to take it."

"Because if I worked eight to ten hours for him, when would I have the energy to work on my own business? I needed time for *my* dreams and *my* goals." The volume of his voice elevated too.

"Well good for you, you achieved your goals, Dante. Look at this place. Congratulations. Our marriage suffered, but who cares, right? Your dreams have come true." She slow-clapped.

Her condescension grated. "As if you cared about our marriage or me. I couldn't give you the life of luxury you wanted, so your father supplied everything for our household because you were unsatisfied living on a poor man's salary."

Her mouth fell open. "Again, *not* true."

"But I understand. It's because of how you were raised. You had everything—servants, money, expensive clothes, cars and couldn't live without those things, even for a little while. I should have known better." He shook his head as a cloud of bitterness enveloped him.

"Fuck. You. You weren't exactly Husband of the Year. You don't get to rewrite history and act like the victim. You didn't give a shit about me. You wanted my family's connections, and when my mother died, you went about your workday like nothing out of the ordinary happened. You weren't there for me."

Her mother, Priscilla Buchanan, passed away suddenly from a brain aneurysm. One minute she was complaining of a headache, the next she had collapsed and was being rushed to the hospital.

"What? You are the one rewriting history. I attended the funeral. You cried in my arms for weeks afterward. I held you while you cried. I was *there*."

Her tears soaked their pillows every night, and he had felt helpless to alleviate her pain. All he could do was curl his body around hers and hold her as she released the anguish of loss.

"At first, yes, but I needed you when I woke up in the middle of the night with pain in my chest, and you were nowhere to be found because you were working late. You did your duty those first few weeks, and then you were done."

"You never said—"

"I lost my mother! I shouldn't have to say. How could you have thought I was over her death?"

Pain coated her words and ripped his heart to pieces.

"I didn't think you were over her death. I assumed you had learned to cope. Is that why you left? Why you told me that you were going to spend a few days with your father and then never came back? One day I came home, and all your things were gone."

Her lips tilted upward as if she was amused, but he saw the bitterness in her smile.

"Do you know how many days it took for you to realize I was gone for good? Three. I remember exactly. I moved out on a Wednesday. You didn't call until Saturday."

Shame burned his cheekbones. He had been consumed with gaining more and more, and Saturday arrived before he noticed her primary toothbrush was missing. She hadn't taken her travel brush. The one she kept in the bathroom was gone. Once he noticed, he rummaged through the drawers. Empty. Checked her closet. Empty.

"You were such a great husband. Well done," Annabelle added with deep sarcasm.

She turned away from him, but Dante moved with lightning speed. As she opened the door, he slammed it shut.

She spun to face him.

"I am not done talking," he said in a low, slow voice.

One hand on the door above her head, he gazed down into her face, noting the mutinous set of her lush mouth and the way her breasts rose and fell with each deep breath.

"*I'm* done. Let me out of here." Her eyes flashed with anger.

"You will leave when this conversation is over."

"And I guess only the great Dante Escarra gets to decide when I leave, is that correct?"

He flashed a grin. "Correct."

If her glare was a sword, he'd be chopped into tiny pieces.

Annabelle stepped away from him with her hands on her hips and went to stand in the middle of the room. "If we're going to talk, let's talk. Let's get everything out in the open, shall we? I want to know why you married me the first time. The real reason."

"Because I loved you." *Worshiped you. Adored you.*

She had consumed him and had been his world. His highs and his lows. Nothing else mattered.

"It's not the real reason, and you know it."

"There was no other reason."

Annabelle laughed in a dry, humorless way. "You can't admit the truth, even to yourself. Here's what I know. You married me because you saw an opportunity to enter the world I occupied. My father and I had connections to people you wanted to be in contact with. That's why you married me, and you took full advantage of those connections. So excuse me if I had doubts about your so-called love for me."

"You doubted my love for you?" Dante had never suspected. He couldn't believe it.

"All I know is what I saw."

"That is ridiculous! Why did *you* marry *me*?"

"I loved you."

"But once we married, you realized being married to a poor man and walking away from the life you'd grown up in was not so great. Is that it? The money, the wealth, the parties. The chauffeur, the servants."

"There you go again making untrue accusations. I never cared about any of those things. I wanted *you*."

"Bull. Shit. What did I have to offer you? I had nothing. No formal education. No fine clothes. I barely spoke English."

She looked at him in shock. "I can't believe that's what you thought of yourself."

Heat tinged his cheekbones. "Then why did you leave?"

"Why would I stay?"

"That is *not* an answer," Dante growled, hanging on to his patience with the thinnest of threads.

She seemed hesitant to respond at first, but then she let out a sigh of resignation. "After Cliffy died, a part of my father died too. H-he didn't see me anymore and nothing mattered. I grew up knowing the heir had passed, and I could never compare to my brother. When I met you, you... made me feel seen. I felt out of place in my own family, but when I was with you... everything fell into place."

He experienced the same emotions with her. His life had been in tumult, but seeing her that day at the restaurant changed his perspective. He ached to capture her laughter and glow. He couldn't believe his good fortune when she agreed to go out with him.

"Eventually, our lives fell apart because you were too busy building your empire, and I didn't fit into your life either."

The hollowed-out sound of her voice caused a twisty ache in his chest.

As a teen in Caracas, he and his crew often courted trouble, and he constantly stressed out his parents. Coming to this country had been a way for him to start anew, change the course of his life, and lift his family out of financial crisis.

"My mother often told me, 'You need to make something of yourself.' That's what I was trying to do, but in the process, I alienated the woman I loved. Maybe I had become too focused on success, but I thought I had more time."

He didn't expect her to bail so soon. Why didn't she give him more *time*?

"You never had to shine shoes, or take odd jobs to pay the bills, or labor for twelve hours in the hot sun with only a thirty-minute break to eat." As he spoke, he moved closer, his voice heavy. "I worked for less than ten dollars an hour and was *grateful*. Before I met you, I shared a two-bedroom apartment with four other people to save money. When I purchased my first property, there were six of us in a three-bedroom because I needed to save for my next purchase. I wanted to give you the life you were familiar with, but I wanted that life too," Dante admitted.

He saw compassion and understanding in her eyes. They had both been lost and reaching out to each other for happiness. Instead, they'd been deeply wounded, leaving each other damaged and scarred.

"What happened to us? How did we fail so miserably?" Annabelle asked in a soft voice.

Dante mulled the question, letting the silence lengthen between them for a time. "We were young and dumb."

The corners of her mouth jerked upward. "Now we're older and dumb?"

They both laughed, quietly at first and then with more energy. The moment of levity was rare between them and expelled the tension and emotion clogging the room.

When they stopped laughing, Annabelle folded her arms across her abdomen. "Thank you... for the perfume bottle. I really mean that. It's beautiful."

"You're welcome."

Neither of them moved.

"I um, I guess I'll go back to my room now."

"I don't think that's a good idea," Dante said, the thickness in his voice betraying his physical response to her.

Annabelle licked her lips, as if they'd suddenly gone dry. "Why not?" she asked in a soft voice.

Dante walked slowly toward her and stopped within reach. "The great Dante Escarra has not given you permission to leave."

❧ 19 ❧

Annabelle froze as Dante prowled closer, heart hammering in her chest with anticipation. She knew what was coming, and deep down, this was what she'd wanted for the longest time.

When his mouth finally closed over hers, she swayed against him and sighed with intense satisfaction. Her arms went immediately around his neck, and their lips pressed together in a hot and needy kiss.

No one kissed like Dante. No one touched her like Dante. She drowned in his mouth, tiny tremors rippling through her as his hands gripped her ass and forced her into deeper contact with his hard length.

They quickly dispensed with their clothes and tumbled onto the huge bed, limbs intertwined and warm flesh gliding against warm flesh as they moved in feverish exploration.

Pulling her on top of him, Dante lay back against the pillows. "Touch me," he whispered.

He guided her hand to slide down his chest to the hardness between his thighs, and Annabelle took delight in hearing him haul a harsh, ragged breath into his lungs. He was hot and warm in the palm of her hand. She stroked him from base to tip, all the while letting her mouth explore the saltiness of his skin. His firm pecs, the rigid peak of an erect nipple, and the fascinating lines making up his abdomen.

His dick sat up straight and erect, thick and beautiful in a base of dark hair. Annabelle licked its full length, watching from the corner of her eye as Dante's fingers curled into the sheets. He didn't make much noise when they made love, but his reactions told the full story. She plucked the mushroomed head between her lips and moaned when she tasted precum. Pulling him deeper, she held him with one hand and slid the other between her thighs, stroking her drenched clit in tandem with the up and down motion of her mouth.

Dante's labored breathing filled her ears, and his clenched fingers yanked the sheets as if he aimed to tear them from the mattress. Her mouth stretched from his girth, and she continued sucking, squeezing, and moaning, high off the knowledge she could bring this powerful, handsome man to the brink of self-control.

His body trembled, signaling he neared release, but one minute Dante was clawing the linens, and the next, he was gripping her long plait.

His dark eyes glittered at her with resolve. "*Ven aquí*," he commanded.

Without waiting for her to move, he hauled her up his body and rolled her onto her back. His weight came down, and his mouth covered hers in a kiss that devoured and demanded with searing intensity.

Dante delivered sucking kisses to her sensitive throat and collarbone, and Annabelle whimpered at the sensation of his firm lips against her heated skin. Lower he went, in between the valley of her breasts.

His warm breath on the underside of her breasts made her nipples tighten. Biting her lip, she twisted against him and closed her eyes, arching her back in a silent plea to pull her nipple into his mouth.

Finally, he gave her what she wanted. Gentle sucking at first, which threatened to drive her mad. He took his time with each breast, paying homage to each achingly swollen dark peak with his tongue. She could hardly stand the gentle pressure, but when he sucked hard, she gasped out loud and sank her nails into his muscled shoulders.

"*Ah, querida, mi cielo, mi reina,*" he said in a guttural voice.

Cupping her mound, he let his fingers play with her clit and stroke the folds of her wet sex. Fisting the sheets, she moved her hips in undulating waves against the movement of his hands. She was dizzy with desire, almost incoherent as he continued to torture her.

Kissing him was not enough. Being touched by him was not enough. Sucking him was not enough. Annabelle needed more and begged for it in a hushed, cracking voice filled with need. But he refused to give her what she wanted, easing lower and taking his time with his exploration.

Dante shaped the curve of her hips with his hands and lingered on the flat plane of her stomach. Then he made her belly quiver as he circled her navel with his tongue and whispered Spanish words of adoration and desire.

He kissed the butterfly tattoo on her hip and gently gnawed the sensitive flesh at the crease of her thighs. Everywhere he touched, electricity crackled under her skin and sparked fire to her nerves.

Dante nudged her legs wider, and her breath hitched in anticipation of his next move. She lay splayed open to him. Her throat tight. Her body rigid. Then his mouth was on her—and his tongue followed. Knowing. Searching. Demanding. That wicked pink snake, as wicked as its owner, glided along her wet slit. Her head tossed from side to side. She could barely stand the sensation of the intimate caress—so deliciously carnal—she became disoriented in the throes of pleasure.

Dante's hands on her hips kept her firmly in place. She couldn't move. She couldn't edge backward to give herself reprieve. She simply had to take what he offered. A careful, calculated tongue-fucking.

She climaxed with one hand against the back of his head and one leg thrown over his shoulder.

He didn't stop.

He continued to devour her until another orgasm tore up her spine, sending her spiraling into ecstasy. Her own hands squeezing her aroused breasts to magnify the effects of the orgasm. It was as if a volcano had erupted inside her body, and she released gasping moans in the aftershocks of the explosion.

When Dante finally lifted his head, she was exhausted. Spent. Boneless and limp.

He kissed his way up her belly to the sensitive spot at the side of her neck.

"*¿Te gusta?*" he asked.

"God yes. *Yes*," Annabelle whispered in a shaky voice.

She wrapped her arms around him and ran her palms up his muscular back. His body was magnificent. Tight muscle covered in smooth skin, all the way down to his tight rear end.

Dante started making love to her again, more slowly this time. There was less urgency as they kissed and caressed each other.

They faced each other, lying on their sides, and Dante pulled one of her legs across his muscular thigh. He inserted a finger into her wet core, and Annabelle bit her lip, toes curling at the gentle intrusion. He followed with another finger and gently pumped them in and out of her, using a slow dragging motion that tortured as much as it titillated.

Unbelievably, her desire built to a boiling point again, and she buried her face in the crook of his neck. "Please, please."

"Please what? Tell me what you want."

"You. Inside me. *Please*." She was shameless. Desperate.

Dante positioned himself above her on both hands. "You are so beautiful when you are like this, with your legs spread and your body wet and begging for mine." He pulled her lower lip between his teeth. "Take it. It's yours."

Never breaking eye contact, Annabelle closed her fingers around his hard erection, and a groan shot from the depths of his throat.

She pulled him lower as she lifted her hips at the same time, and Dante sank his body into hers. Her slickly aroused sex accepted him with ease. She welcomed his possession, her muscles tightening and fitting him like a silken glove.

A helpless cry escaped her lips. Finally, he was inside her again, and she felt unbelievably full.

She had never experienced anything so exquisitely good in her life. Dante dipped his head to her shoulder and as he moved, his soft groans vibrated against her skin. Gripping him, she sank her nails into his broad back and lifted her hips to deepen his penetration.

"Oh, yes—yes," she whispered, gasping at the strength of each thrust.

Annabelle's mouth fell open on a silent cry, and she folded her legs around his waist.

She clung to him as he moved harder and faster. His hands fisted in the soft sheets, and his breath came out in harsh bursts of passion.

An orgasm rose from her loins and clawed its way up her back. She screamed aloud, uninhibited and exultant as she drowned in wave after wave of pleasure. Pressing her nose to Dante's strong throat, she inhaled his sweat damp skin and the earthiness of his cologne, clamping an arm around his neck to bring them closer.

He plunged deeper, his hips undulating in a sexy grind against hers and drawing out another shuddering climax. Squeezing her eyes closed, Annabelle screamed again and clawed his back.

With savage, hard strokes, he climaxed too and let out a

grunt as he expelled air from his lungs and his heavy body collapsed on top of hers.

❦

DID THAT REALLY HAPPEN?

A quick glance to her left, and Annabelle confirmed she was, in fact, lying next to Dante, which further confirmed they did, in fact, have sex multiple times.

In deep sleep, he rolled toward her, burying half his face in the soft pillows and draping an arm across her hips.

He still does that? she thought.

He used to make the same move when they were married the first time, as if unconsciously making sure—while in deep sleep—that she remained beside him. A smile touched the corners of her mouth at the thought of thirty-two-year-old Dante needing reassurance.

Even at twenty-one, without the trappings of wealth, he had been a force to be reckoned with, confident in his abilities to succeed. Age had made him sexier, and he carried a worldly maturity in a way he didn't back then.

They were both different. Could they make their relationship work this time? She shouldn't want more, but the thoughts plagued her.

Annabelle stifled a yawn. Sex had made her work up an appetite.

Carefully, she extricated herself from the bed and pulled on her pajamas. Tiptoeing out of the room, she went downstairs to the spacious kitchen and checked the refrigerator. Viviana always kept cut up fresh fruit in the fridge. She made a small plate with pineapple and kiwi and smeared a generous portion of cream cheese on a toasted bagel with smoked salmon. Standing at the counter in the dim kitchen, she hummed to herself as she devoured the satisfying late-night snack.

As she was eating, Dante's strong arms wrapped around her waist from behind, and he buried his face in her neck.

"I woke up, and you were gone," he murmured.

Annabelle melted into his embrace. He wore only his boxers, and she delighted in the warmth exuding from his warm chest.

"I was hungry. Want some?" she asked.

He grunted and opened his mouth. Over her shoulder, she slipped the last of her bagel and salmon between his lips.

"That was good. Is there any more?" he asked.

"That was the last piece. Here." She placed a piece of pineapple in his mouth. He sucked in the fruit and swirled his tongue against her fingertips.

The action reminded her of the swirl of his tongue between her legs.

"You're so nasty," she whispered.

Dante chuckled. "I am only eating the pineapple you gave me."

"Mhmm. You know what you're doing."

Eating quietly in the dark, they consumed all the fruit with Dante flush against her back and her body leaning into his bare chest. They were as comfortable and relaxed as if they had repeated the very same position dozens of times before.

When they finished, Dante trailed the tip of his nose along the curve of her neck and sucked her bare shoulder. With a quiet grunt, he slid his hands higher and cupped her breasts.

"Mmm." Annabelle moaned softly, letting her head fall back and her body arch into his large hands as he squeezed.

His teeth tugged at the corner of her mouth, and she tilted her head to give him better access to her lips.

"We should go upstairs," she whispered, reaching back to caress his jaw.

"We should," he agreed, without moving.

He continued to massage her breasts through the thin top, pebbling her nipples and making her horny again.

Frustrated, she turned in his arms and traced the hard line of his jaw with her fingertips. Her thumb grazed his beautiful lower lip. They locked eyes, and then she kissed him, immediately opening her mouth to touch her tongue to his.

Dante groaned and edged her toward the fridge. Cold steel hit her shoulders.

"Dante, we can't. One of the servants might see us," Annabelle whispered, though excitement laced her voice.

"They never come in here this late at night."

"How do you know?"

"I know."

His strong fingers collared her throat as he pinned her to the fridge, and she whimpered. When he lowered his head to hers, she became lost in the darkness of his eyes.

"You will move into the master bedroom tomorrow," he said softly.

Not a question. Simply a statement of what would be done.

He dragged his tongue up the side of her neck. "Say yes."

"Yes."

"Good girl." Hunger deepened and roughened his voice.

Winding her long braid around his fist, he gently tugged her head back and sucked her left nipple through the fabric of her pajamas. Her knees almost gave way, and she clung to him.

"My wife," he said with a deep growl, almost as if he were amazed by the fact.

Then he dragged aside the crotch of her shorts and filled her with his length. Lifting her against the cold appliance, he thrust over and over into her until they both climaxed, Dante groaning in satisfaction and Annabelle stifling a scream in the side of his neck.

20

Nolson Hilderbrandt's grand estate consisted of a Neoclassical designed mansion, horse stables, and elaborate gardens which included fruit trees, located twenty miles outside of Houston on ten acres of wooded land. As Annabelle and Dante approached in the black Lincoln Navigator he'd hired, the long driveway to the front door gave the impression that they were out in the middle of nowhere.

The car approached the front of the house, and Dante shifted in the seat, the knowledge that he was finally getting an audience with Nolson hitting him square in the chest. He'd waited a long time for this day and intended to make the best of it.

Clifton had declined this year's invitation, so Dante and Annabelle were attending the party without him. When they exited the car, she curled her fingers around his biceps. Tonight, her loose-fitting ivory dress highlighted the golden tone of her skin. The elegant design had been created by Lacey and swept low around her ankles, leaving her arms bare. In her hand, she carried a white bejeweled clutch and wore her hair in an intricate chignon with diamond clips holding it in place.

He'd donned a white dress shirt, a tailored black jacket, and matching black slacks, pairing the look with a modestly priced black and white luxury watch.

Upon entering the house, he and Annabelle strolled across a red carpet that presented the pathway through the house. They encountered familiar faces from the real estate world and smiled at and greeted each person in turn, accepting words of congratulations from those who hadn't attended the wedding but knew they'd remarried. They also passed by rooms where guests lounged on plush sofas and chatted with each other as they noshed on canapés and sipped mixed drinks offered by the circulating servers dressed in black.

Soft jazz music interspersed with sounds of laughter beckoned them to a huge room transformed into a casino. The space was illuminated by golden lights which reflected off the mirrored walls. Guests crowded around a blackjack table, baccarat table, roulette wheels, and two poker tables at opposite ends of the room. There was also a wheel of fortune, where guests placed bets for specific items, cheering when they won and groaning when they lost.

The five-piece band of jazz performers were out on the terrace, where additional invitees sipped on drinks and smoked cigars. This was the kind of world Dante had only dreamed about when he shined shoes early in the morning and then had to rush off to his second job, where he toiled in the hot sun as a laborer.

"Hello! Welcome!" Khuyen, Nolson's twenty-five-year-old wife greeted them with bright, happy eyes.

Khuyen was Vietnamese American, a member of the large number of Vietnamese who lived in Houston. Her family owned several restaurants in the city, and apparently Nolson had been dining at one of them when he saw her and was smitten. His wife passed years ago, and Khuyen was not the first time Dante had heard his name linked with another woman. It was the first time, however, he had openly dated any of them. Whether their connection resulted from love or not, Khuyen and Nolson were married within six months and celebrated their third anniversary this past January.

Khuyen and Annabelle exchanged air kisses.

"I try never to miss your annual party. I heard the casino night theme was your idea, which I love, by the way," Annabelle gushed.

She was in her element and was a sight to behold. She put the "social" in socialite.

"You're too kind," Khuyen said, looking pleased. "I thought I'd shake things up a bit. Thank goodness Nolson was open to the idea." Her long black hair fell in body waves and spilled onto her bare shoulders, exposed in a strapless gold dress with a huge silver and gold bow over her breasts.

"This is my husband, Dante Escarra."

"Nice to meet you, but of course I know who you are," Khuyen said, extending her hand for Dante to shake. "I wish we could have made the wedding. We were traveling out of the country. Congratulations to you both. By the way, Nolson has been very impressed with your—as he calls it—meteoric rise in real estate."

"I'm honored to meet you. I've heard only good things," Dante lied smoothly.

As she was the same age as Nolson's children, they were not pleased, and there were rumors of infighting among the family because of her presence.

Khuyen blushed. "Why, thank you."

"Where is Nolson?" Dante asked.

"Around here somewhere," she replied airily, waving her hand in the general direction of the baccarat table. "Do you mind if I steal Annabelle for a minute?"

"Not at all."

"Good, because I heard the board at Buchanan & Buchanan is selecting you as the new CEO at this month's meeting." Khuyen arched an eyebrow.

"Oh, that. It's not a done deal yet," Annabelle said with false modesty.

"I want to hear all about it. Dante, please make yourself at home. You, come with me," Khuyen said to Annabelle.

Before they walked away, Dante slipped an arm around Annabelle's waist and pressed his lips to her cheek. She smelled like heaven, and having her soft body against his made him stifle an involuntary groan. "I'll see you later, *querida*. Try not to lose all our money."

She flashed a smile. "I won't, darling. Though there's plenty more where that came from."

Khuyen sighed. "Newlyweds. Y'all get on my nerves." Then she laughed and looped her arm around Annabelle's.

Dante watched them walk away. The kiss had not been solely for appearances. The situation at home was better. They'd had sex almost every night in the past couple of weeks and ate dinner together on a regular basis, their conversations no longer stilted and awkward. She laughed more. She smiled more.

The perfume bottle he purchased in Las Vegas had pleased her more than he realized. After she moved into his bedroom, he noticed she placed it on the vanity tray with her favorite bottles. Her pleasure created a warm sensation in the pit of his stomach. He wanted more of her smiles. More of her pleasure. More of her happiness.

Such was his dilemma. Their marriage was supposed to be temporary, and ideally, they should be living separate lives, but he was going through an internal struggle. On the one hand, he didn't trust Annabelle. She had broken his heart and trampled on his pride ten years ago. However, they were both different now. Older. He had money. He could offer her a better life than they had before.

Mierda. What was he thinking? Before Annabelle waltzed into his office, he never contemplated getting married again, so this train of thought was ridiculous and unwelcome.

Dante shook his head and went to purchase some chips. Then he made his way over to the roulette table. After several spins, where he ultimately lost over one thousand dollars, he spotted Nolson entering the room. He was in conversation with two women, nodding his head to whatever they were saying. Dressed in a three-piece suit with pinstripes, he wore a Rolex on his wrist. The vintage kind handed down from his father or grandfather.

He was in his late forties, with salt-and-pepper hair and beard and a softening body caused by the advance of age. Several more people gathered around, with Nolson the center of attention, nodding sagely from time to time and speaking equally with his mouth and hands.

Dante wanted to talk to him, but he wanted to do so privately. Almost an hour later, the opportunity presented itself when the crowd around the older man dispersed.

Before Nolson could walk away, Dante approached and extended his hand. "Mr. Hilderbrandt, I'm Dante Escarra."

Nolson shook his hand, and the corners of his mouth tilted upward. "The great Dante Escarra. I know exactly who you are. How are you liking married life again? To the same woman, no less."

"So far so good."

Nolson chuckled. "Personally, I never expected to get married again, but when love hits you, what can you do?" He shrugged.

"True. Have you been out on the links lately?" Dante asked. Nolson enjoyed golfing, one of the few recreational activities he engaged in outside of work.

"Not lately," Nolson lamented. "I don't get out on the course as much as I used to, which is a shame. I've made many business deals out there."

The Hilderbrandts had earned their fortune in chemical manufacturing, using oil as a raw material to produce fertilizers, pesticides, and other products. Though by no means poor, because of fierce competition in recent years, they'd lost market share and their fortunes had shrunk. But they were a wealthy family by any standard and demanded respect because of their extended roots in Texas.

Hilderbrandt Plaza was an anomaly in their portfolio and represented a time when they wielded more power and influence in business and politics.

Nolson took a glass of wine from one of the passing servers. "Your reputation precedes you. I've observed how well you've done in recent years, and I'm very impressed."

"That's good to hear, because you have something I want." He didn't see any reason to beat around the bush.

"Oh?"

"Hilderbrandt Plaza. I heard it's for sale."

Nolson sipped his wine, watching Dante over the rim. Dante held his gaze without flinching.

"I know you're quite the shark," Nolson finally said.

"Shark might be a harsh term," Dante said slowly.

"Is it? You own quite a bit of Houston, and according to credible rumors you're buying up parts of the Midwest in anticipation of a surge in coming years." He leaned closer to Dante. "What's your secret?"

Dante fit a smile to his lips. "Patience. She has been very good to me. But I don't want to bombard you with business talk at your party. This is a festive occasion. Why don't we have lunch in the next week or two at Prosciutto?"

He had once read an article where they reported the tiny Italian restaurant was one of Nolson's favorite places to dine, and he mourned its popularity in recent years, which made securing a reservation difficult. Dante hoped that was still the case.

"Prosciutto? They're booked solid for at least a month," Nolson grumbled.

"Not for me. I own their lease," Dante said smoothly. The owners didn't make exceptions for anyone else but him.

Nolson chuckled and eyed him with renewed interest. "I

haven't had their gnocchi in months. If you can arrange lunch there, I'll definitely join you, and we can talk about the plaza."

"I can arrange lunch," Dante confirmed.

"Good. Get in touch with my secretary, Marla, on Monday. She's here somewhere. I'll tell her to expect your call."

"Sounds good. I'll be in touch on Monday."

21

Sipping white wine, Annabelle watched Dante from across the room. Her gaze easily found him because of his height. He stood taller than many of the people there, with his midnight hair looking brilliant under the lights.

His clothes fit snug but not tight—showcasing his taut body in a black jacket molded over his broad shoulders and black pants hinting at the powerful, muscular thighs underneath. No tie, and the open collar of his shirt revealed his tanned throat.

He hadn't changed much from the young man she married ages ago. One who'd balked at every instance of wearing a tie and jacket.

"Another event that requires a tie?" Dante's *gaze shot toward the ceiling in annoyance.*

"It won't kill you," Annabelle *admonished, working on a Windsor knot on his paisley tie. "It's an evening party, and all the men will be dressed in suits."*

"We are in Houston, in the summer, and I really do not care what people think of me."

"You should care. These are the people you'll be doing business with in the future."

His lips flattened. He couldn't argue because she was right. "One of these days, I am going to be so rich, no one would dare question me when I show up dressed however the hell I want," he grumbled.

"Until then..." She smoothed the tie over his chest and stepped back to examine her handiwork. "You play by the rules, or you don't get invited to the games."

His conversation with Nolson had ended several minutes ago. She was no body-language expert, but if she had to guess, she'd say it went well.

She hadn't heard from Albert again, and soon she'd have the CEO position locked down. Whatever Dante said to him must have stuck.

Very shortly, Dante might be able to purchase Hilderbrandt Plaza. They'd both get what they wanted out of this marriage, and then they'd only have to wait until the time ran out on their agreement.

One year.

The situation at home was certainly better since they had sex, but she felt more uncertain than ever about her relationship with Dante. She had moved into the master bedroom, and they were screwing like rabbits. Night after night, she wrapped her legs around him and welcomed his drugging kisses and the hard thrusts of his body into hers.

But what exactly were they *doing*?

"You're frowning," a male voice said close to her ear.

The statement came from Vance Greenfeld, an old friend and chronic flirt who was rumored to have affairs with the married women he coached at the tennis club his family owned.

"Am I?" Annabelle tossed a mildly flirtatious glance his way. Vance loved women, period. He didn't have a type and didn't care about age.

He inclined his dark head, amusement in his eyes. "Mhmm. Frowning at your husband. Please tell me there's trouble in paradise, so I can have my shot."

Vance was an odd mixture of attractive but average. He didn't turn heads, but he was always dressed in high-end suits and wore his dark hair parted on the side and combed into a neat style. At a few years older than Annabelle, he could be married by now but preferred the life of a perpetual bachelor.

"We're newlyweds enjoying the honeymoon period. Sorry to disappoint you, but there's no trouble in paradise." Because there was no paradise, but at least the animosity was gone, and they had learned to live harmoniously.

Just last night, Dante had pinned her against the wall in the shower, palms flat and the tips of her breasts tight against the rigid, cold marble. Water poured down on them from above as he plowed her from behind until her moans echoed in the glass enclosure, both of them climaxing at the same time.

She suppressed a delicious shiver at the memory.

"I haven't seen you at the club in a while. Have you given up tennis?" Vance asked.

"Temporarily. My weekends and days are busy."

He leaned closer with a leer. "How are your nights?"

A heavy hand landed on his shoulder, and he winced.

Dante's dark eyes glittered at her from behind Vance.

"Should I be concerned that you're standing too close to my wife?" Dante positioned himself beside Annabelle.

Dangerous, raw power emanated from him. He sounded teasingly pleasant, but the loaded question definitely held a threat.

He slid an arm around her waist. Hip to hip, she experienced the warmth of his body all the way down to her knees.

Vance laughed nervously. "Not at all. In fact, Annabelle confirmed you're enjoying the honeymoon period."

"How did that come up in conversation?" Dante continued in the same overly pleasant voice.

Blood drained from Vance's face. "I, uh—"

"He was asking about marriage, and I gave him a little advice about keeping the excitement in the relationship long after the ceremony. Of course, I'm no expert since we're newlyweds, but I gave him a couple of tips. Isn't that right, Vance?"

"Absolutely. Very helpful." He nodded vigorously.

Dante didn't reply, and she could tell by the stillness of his body that he didn't believe a word she said. He silently watched Vance—whose eyes darted around the room—until awkward silence cloaked the air around the three of them.

Dante had no problem standing in discomfort, but she was not as blessed to have the same attitude he did. Unable to handle the uncomfortable quiet any longer, Annabelle spoke first.

"I guess I'll see you on the courts as soon as I clear my schedule," she said.

Vance took the lifeline she tossed him. "Definitely. We'll catch up soon. I'll see you both... uh, later."

He scurried away, and Annabelle took the opportunity to separate from Dante.

"Was that necessary?" she asked, smiling through her teeth.

"We had an agreement, *querida*. We agreed neither of us would embarrass the other."

"Yes. We did."

"Then why were you flirting with him?"

"I wasn't flirting—"

"I could see you across the room. You were flirting with each other, in the middle of a party, only weeks after our wedding. What do you think people will say?"

"Don't worry, Dante. No one would dare question whether or not we're happy. I'm sure everyone here realizes how lucky I am." Her smile tightened as she gazed up at him.

He bent low to whisper, so when he spoke, his breath brushed the shell of her ear. "Do not embarrass me, and I won't embarrass you. If I'm not satisfying you, all you have to do is say you want more."

He trailed a finger down the inside of her arm, and goosebumps popped onto her skin.

"Could your ego be any bigger?" she whispered the words against the corner of his mouth.

Laughter climbed up his strong throat, and his dimples made an appearance. "*Querida*, really, all you have to do is ask." Dante placed a hand low on her back. His hand was so low, two of his fingers touched her ass.

He dropped an unexpected kiss to her cheek and let his hand fall away, purposely copping a feel of her bottom as he did, and then sauntered away. Bastard. Now she was horny in the middle of casino night, her heart beating fast and her loins heavy with want.

A few feet away, Khuyen watched her with a knowing smirk.

Annabelle shrugged, smiling like any happily married woman would who had been caught having a flirty moment with her spouse.

🐾

DANTE FOUND VANCE IN ONE OF THE OTHER ROOMS, standing in a corner alone, texting on his phone. There were only a few other people in there. A man and women had their heads close together while they talked. Another man sat in an armchair talking in low tones on the phone.

He thought about Annabelle, elegant and exquisite-looking in a white dress billowing around her with each movement and offering teasing glimpses of her shapely figure every time the lightweight fabric settled against her body. He made his way over to the other man with anger percolating inside him and trying to claw its way out.

Vance looked up, and when he saw Dante, surprise filled his eyes. "Hi." He glanced around the room—either looking for Annabelle or in a state of confusion as to why Dante had come over to speak to him.

"How are you?" Dante asked.

"Great. You?"

"Excellent."

"Um, great party, isn't it?"

Dante's gaze narrowed a fraction. He obviously made Vance

nervous, and the other man had a hard time figuring out what to say to him.

"Do you think my wife is beautiful?" he asked.

"Huh?"

"You heard me. Do you find Annabelle beautiful?"

Vance laughed nervously, and then he shrugged. "I don't know why you would be asking me that question."

"I know your reputation. You... get around, so to speak."

"I'm a man. I'm sure you understand—"

"No, I don't. I don't understand anyone who does not respect the vows of marriage."

Vance's cheeks turned pink. "Excuse me, I have to go."

Dante pressed a hand to his chest and held him in place. "I'm not done talking. Do not walk away from me."

One of the reasons people referred to him as the devil was because of his confrontational style. He didn't do hints or beating around the bush. He got straight to the point.

He inched closer, and Vance swallowed.

To anyone else, they appeared to be two friends having an intense conversation. "I know you want my wife. My question is, are you foolish enough to make a play for her, to try to seduce her? *My* wife. I don't think there is a man alive who would do something so... dangerously stupid. Because any man who does that must know that I, Dante Escarra, would destroy everything he knows and loves. I would leave nothing but charred Earth in the wake of my rage at any man who *thinks* he could possibly take what is mine. I'm a very rich man, Vance, but nothing I own is more valuable, more precious to me, than my wife. I never want to see you trying to get cozy with *my wife* ever again. I have a very long memory, and I'm a patient man." He placed a hand on Vance's shoulder and squeezed. "I am warning you, for your own good, and I don't make idle threats. Do not fuck with me. You will live to regret it."

He locked eyes with Vance, so he'd know he meant every one

of those softly spoken words, and there was no mistaking the fear in Vance's eyes.

Satisfied the message he delivered was clear and understood, Dante removed his hand and walked out of the room. Famished, he went in search of food to eat.

But the gravity of his own words lingered like smoke at the periphery of his brain. The most important thing in his life wasn't a thing at all, wasn't a possession. How ironic. No matter how much money he made or property he owned, Annabelle was the greatest prize of all—the vibrant, intelligent woman he had fallen in love with years ago.

And was clearly in danger of falling in love with again.

22

The silence in the back of the black SUV was deafening. Dante sensed Annabelle wanted to say something, but for the moment, she held her tongue. For his part, he didn't need to talk. He welcomed silence and thrived in situations where others were uncomfortable.

The driver pulled up to the front, where light poured through the glass doors. He helped Annabelle down from the vehicle, and Dante climbed out the other side. The driver waited for him as he rounded the vehicle.

"Will there be anything else this evening, Mr. Escarra?"

"No, thank you. Good night."

"Good night, sir."

Dante followed Annabelle into the house.

She stopped at the bottom of the staircase and faced him. "Did you say something to Vance tonight?"

"Finally, she speaks."

"Don't be sarcastic. Answer the question."

"Something like what?" Dante asked, walking past her. He heard her following.

"Did you threaten him?"

"Yes."

"You're not even denying it!" she exclaimed.

Dante entered their bedroom and shrugged out of his jacket. "Why would I deny the truth? I threatened him, and I'm not ashamed, though I'm surprised he told you. Hmm... I must not have intimidated him enough."

"I joined a conversation he was already in with two other people and noticed he barely made eye contact with me. I cornered him later, and he said you and he had a talk and he needed to stay away from me. He looked absolutely terrified. I practically had to drag the rest of the information out of him. He glanced over his shoulder every few seconds as if he was afraid the devil himself would appear and haul him to the depths of hell. "

"Drag it out of him? Cute."

"Nothing about what you did was cute."

"I meant you're cute when you're protective of your piece-of-shit friends."

She muttered a curse under her breath, and he hid his amusement because it would only inflame her anger.

"Dante, you can't go around threatening people."

"Why not?" He tossed his jacket on the plush bench at the foot of the bed.

Resting a hand on her hip, she stared at him in disbelief. "Because it's... it's not done."

"You know who you married. You're my wife." His tone was firm and possessive.

"Everyone knows that."

"Apparently, not everyone. Your friend thinks there's a gray area." He started on his cuffs.

"Vance is a friend, that's all."

"A friend who wants to screw you. Stop pretending you don't know what he wants. Maybe you've resisted in the past, I don't know." Dante shrugged. "Maybe he finds you more appealing now you have a ring on your finger. I don't care about his reasons. I only care that he knows I know what he's up to. *Bueno.*

This conversation is over."

Annabelle blinked, temporarily speechless. "Excuse me? Did you dismiss me?"

"Yes, because this conversation is over."

"I am not a goddamn child, Dante."

"No, you're not, but you're also not going to change my mind and make me feel guilt or remorse about how I handled the situation with Vance. He knows where I stand now. He knows what line he can't cross, and if he crosses it again, there will be consequences."

"There will be..." Annabelle stopped, biting her lip. "Are you listening to yourself?"

"I know exactly what I said. I know what I told Vance, and I know what I told you. It's late. Time for bed."

He went into his closet and allowed himself a soft laugh. Annabelle had to be the most infuriating woman alive. Did she really think he would allow Vance or any man to hit on her? The *hijo de puta* was lucky all Dante did was talk. In his younger days, he much preferred to settle disputes with his fists.

Dante removed his dress shirt and undershirt, balled them up, and tossed them in the hamper in his large dressing room. Unbuckling his belt, he removed his pants and tossed them on top of the pile. He exited into the bedroom to find Annabelle waiting in the middle of the floor with her arms crossed over her chest. Her sexy mouth was set in a rebellious stance, and her entire body set in rigid lines of coiled tension.

"You're still dressed," he said.

"Because I'm not done talking to you." She averted her eyes from his hair sprinkled chest and bare thighs.

"*Ay, Dios.* You never know when to stop. That was one of our problems before. Our arguments should have lasted ten minutes, but because of your stubbornness, they could go on for ten days."

Her mouth fell open. "That is *not* true."

"It is true." Her refusal to back down made his blood spike

with desire. "Are you sure you want to continue this conversation?"

"Yes!" she answered, sounding exasperated.

"You can pretend to be angry, but I see the way you look at me. You're almost ready, aren't you?"

"You pompous—"

Dante sauntered closer, forcing her gaze higher. "Shh. *Cállate la boca, mi reina.* I will give you what you want."

Her arms fell to her sides. "You can't tell the queen to be quiet."

"Oh, but I can. Because I am the king." He outlined her lips with the tip of his tongue.

She laughed, as if she couldn't help it. "God, I hate you."

He plucked her plump bottom lip between his teeth. "But you like how I make you feel."

Desire wrapped him in a thorny caress and abraded his skin. Pressing his lips to hers, he kissed her with feeling. She moaned and twisted her arms around his neck, and he devoured her for an eternity before backing her toward the bed.

"Let's get you out of this," Dante said huskily, pulling the filmy dress over her head.

He stopped for a moment to appreciate the sexy La Perla lingerie underneath. White lace cupped her breasts—the contrast of the stark color against her golden-brown skin making him harder than steel. He trailed a finger along the edge of the matching white lace thong hanging from her hips.

"You are so sexy," he breathed, molding her hips in his hands and smoothing up her torso to cup her breasts.

Annabelle lay back on the bed and popped the front clasp, freeing her caramel-colored areola and nipples to his hungry gaze. Bending over her, he licked one taut peak and then the other. She sighed and arched into him, cupping the back of his head to smash his face against her soft flesh.

He had never met another woman who set his world on fire the way she did. Every woman since Annabelle had paled in comparison. They didn't have her appetite, and they didn't make his blood boil at the slightest touch.

They stripped naked, and he climbed on top of her on the bed. Pulling one succulent nipple into his mouth, he worried the hard tip with his tongue and teeth until she was moaning and twisting beneath him uncontrollably.

He took his time making love to her, the provocative twisting of her body and her sharp inhales letting him know which licks and kisses she enjoyed the most.

He massaged her swollen breasts and sucked her hard nipples until she begged him to stop. Stretching her hands above her head, he joined their bodies and rocked her with rhythmic thrusts.

Soft, mewling gasps filled his ears until ecstasy tore through them both and the volume of her cries increased, right before they collapsed in a heap of ragged breathing and damp skin.

23

Annabelle was a bundle of nerves. The board was meeting later than usual tonight. Meanwhile, Lacey was having her first fashion show to publicize her fall line. Annabelle had intended to go alone, but she and Dante were getting along so well, she invited him at the last minute to be her escort.

To her mild surprise, he said yes, and she secretly looked forward to the night out with an embarrassing amount of excitement. She wore a floor length olive skirt and backless cream top with long sleeves, both of which were Lacey creations. She slipped her feet into platform shoes with thick heels and finished up by spraying her pulse points with a favorite fragrance.

Leaving her hair down and straight, she tucked one side behind her left ear while the other side fell across her brow and partially covered her face. After placing a Coach purse in the crook of her arm, she exited the bedroom.

At the same time, Dante came out of his dressing room wearing all black—black long-sleeved shirt, black jacket, black slacks, black shoes.

"You look incredible," he said, blatant male appreciation in his gaze. "Are you ready to go?"

"Yes."

Within minutes, they were in the back of the black Lincoln SUV with Dante's favorite driver and on their way to the venue.

"Have you heard from your father yet?" Dante asked.

Annabelle shook her head. "Not yet." Why did the board meeting have to take place tonight, the same night as Lacey's event?

Depending on their agenda, the meeting could run late, which meant she might not find out what the board had decided until after the show. She couldn't keep her phone turned on during the event, and she didn't want to constantly check for missed calls during the show.

Dante took her hand, and the reassuring warmth of his touch calmed her. "You have nothing to worry about. The board will vote in your favor."

She nodded, grateful for his positive remark.

She glanced down at their hands clasped together on the leather seat. The new unspoken understanding between them caused feelings of anger and resentment to all but disappear. She and Dante regularly ate dinner together, and if he was running late to get home, he called. What a difference a few months had made. Hell, a few weeks.

Annabelle's cell phone rang, piercing the quiet dark of the vehicle. Dante twisted his head to look at her and squeezed her hand. She held her breath for a second before pulling the device from her purse. Her father was calling.

She swallowed down the ball of nerves that leapt into her throat. This was it. She would soon learn if she was going to take over the CEO position and keep the jobs of everyone at the company secure, or if they'd all be jeopardized by the board turning down her father's recommendation.

"Hello?"

"Hi, honey. Where are you?" He sounded upbeat. A good sign.

"I'm on the way to Lacey's fashion show." She kept her voice calm and natural though the speed of her heart had tripled and banged against the wall of her chest.

"Oh, I forgot the show was taking place tonight. Well, I hope you're sitting down because I have good news."

Annabelle squeezed her eyes shut.

"The board agreed with my recommendation, and you're going to be the next CEO of Buchanan & Buchanan!"

She opened her mouth wide and let out a silent scream, doubling over and shaking with excitement. When she straightened, Dante looked at her with a line of concern creasing his brow, but when he saw her wide smile, the worry dissipated.

"Thank you, Daddy. You gave me the best news I've heard in a long time."

"I thought you'd like to hear it," Clifton said with a chuckle. "Enjoy your night. Tell Lacey that I wish her the best. You and I should talk soon. I'm ready to step down immediately, and we need to discuss logistics, including moving you into your new office."

She covered her face, slumping against the seat in disbelief. "I'll call you tomorrow?"

"Sounds good, honey. Congratulations."

"Thank you." Annabelle hung up and bit her lip. "I can't believe it."

"We knew this would happen," Dante said.

His face no longer contained the harsh lines they did at the beginning of their marriage. Was she softer too?

"I will continue the Buchanan legacy. *Me.* A woman," Annabelle said in wonderment.

She didn't have much time to wallow in her newfound success because the driver pulled up to the venue. Fashion and local media hovered outside as cars arrived, and they snapped photos and jostled for position to get the best shots of the people arriving.

"She has quite a crowd," Dante murmured.

"Her publicist sent out a lot of invitations, and Lacey put in months of hard work," Annabelle explained.

The driver hopped out of the vehicle and came around to her side.

"Well, I guess I can celebrate later." She slipped from the back of the vehicle.

"Annabelle! Annabelle! This way!"

Dante sauntered off and left her in the midst of the fray. Though he was well-known, his notoriety was limited to the business sector. She was a local celebrity because of the years she'd spent courting media attention when she'd been a young socialite enjoying her father's money.

"Why was it important for you to be here tonight?" a male reporter asked, shoving a microphone in her face.

She paused to answer the question. "Lacey and I have been friends for a long time, so there was never a question of whether or not I would attend tonight. She has always had my support, and tonight is no different."

"Are you wearing one of her designs?" a woman asked.

"Yes, from the summer line." Annabelle turned in a slow circle, and cameras flashed to capture all the angles.

Posing with her back to the reporters, she showed off her bare back, making eye contact over her shoulder. When she thought they'd taken enough photos, she smiled. "I better get inside now."

"How is married life?" someone yelled from the back.

Annabelle kept the smile on her face. "Better the second time around."

She left them with those words and walked to where Dante waited. As she approached, he placed a hand at the small of her back, and they made their way into the venue.

Lacey had reserved a spot for them at the front next to the

stage. An usher guided her and Dante to their seats, and as she sat down, Annabelle nodded at a few familiar faces around her. Almost every seat was occupied.

"I'm so excited for Lacey. She deserves all this attention, and I know her designs are going to make a big splash," she said.

Dante stretched his arm along the back of her chair, and she leaned into the warmth emitted by their contact.

"Did you help her finance this?"

His breath brushed her ear, and her body heated.

Annabelle shook her head. "She did everything herself. Fundraising, finding space, everything. She took advantage of social media and hooked up with influencers to get the word out. She insisted that if she wasn't going to get help from her parents that she didn't want my help. Of course, she also had the money from her trust fund, so this wasn't entirely a bootstrapped endeavor."

"Of course not," Dante said with humor.

"Don't judge."

"No judgment," he insisted, though the corners of his mouth lifted higher.

Annabelle shot a sideways glance at him. "Thank you for coming," she said quietly.

His hand massaged the back of her neck beneath her hair. "Did you doubt that I would?"

"Maybe, a little. This isn't exactly the kind of event I thought you'd attend."

"It's not exactly the kind of thing I normally attend, but I thought it might be interesting. At the very least, I can say I once attended a fashion show."

"You can finally cross it off your list."

"It was at the very top, and I worried I would never have the opportunity to do that. Thank goodness for Lacey."

Annabelle covered her mouth as she laughed. "No need to be sarcastic," she said.

He shot her an amused look, and her insides melted. They

were definitely getting along better. Teasing, laughing—which reminded her of the early days of their first marriage. When they split, she eventually resigned herself to life without him, but in retrospect, she'd only been a shell of herself for years. Her life had been empty. A piece of her had been missing.

Now they were together she fully understood what she had given up when she walked out ten years ago.

"Ms. Buchanan, may I take a picture of you and your husband?" the in-house photographer asked. Photos of prominent attendees could be used in promotional materials later.

"Yes, I don't mind." Annabelle glanced at Dante, and he nodded his agreement.

She leaned closer to him, and his hand cupped her shoulder. The photographer took several snaps and then thanked them before moving on.

Finally, the lights dimmed, and the MC came out on stage. The show was about to begin.

❦

WHEN THE SHOW ENDED, DANTE AND ANNABELLE IDLED NEAR the door at the front of the stage. A three-minute standing ovation had followed Lacey and the models walking out for the runway finale. Her designs were fresh and innovative, and Annabelle believed this time her friend had chosen the correct career path.

When she exited into the auditorium, Annabelle rushed over to give her a hug.

"The show was amazing! I'm so proud of you," she said to Lacey.

"Really? Thank you. I was extremely nervous." She let out a long exhale. "Thank you both for coming. I can't believe I finally did it." Her eyes were bright with tears.

"I always knew you could."

"You're the best."

They hugged again.

Dante's phone rang. He frowned at the screen. "Excuse me. I need to take this call."

As he walked away, Annabelle squeezed Lacey's hand. "What's next? Paris? Milan? New York?"

Lacey groaned. "I don't know. My producer and publicist are working on booking other events. We'll see. But what about you? Have you heard anything yet?"

Annabelle nodded. "Right before we arrived, Daddy called and said the board voted to install me as the next CEO."

Lacey's eyes widened, and she squealed. She pulled Annabelle into a hug. "Oh my goodness, that's wonderful! It's a great night for both of us."

Annabelle nodded.

Lacey lowered her voice. "Any update on Dante's meeting with Nolson?"

Annabelle glanced over her shoulder. He was talking on the phone, head bent in an intense conversation. "They have lunch together next week. Keep your fingers crossed everything goes well."

Lacey's eyes sparkled with interest. "You sound way more invested than I would have expected. How are things between the two of you?"

"Our relationship is better, actually. Much better," Annabelle admitted.

"But...?"

She glanced over her shoulder again to make sure Dante wasn't approaching. "I feel as if we're back to what we were doing when we first got married. Sure the sex is great, but..."

"Great sex is not a bad thing."

"I know," Annabelle said with a laugh, "but..."

"You want more," Lacey guessed.

She nodded, then her skin flushed with embarrassment. "This isn't the time or place to have this conversation."

Lacey touched her arm. "Can I give you some advice—

coming from someone who is terrible in relationships and doesn't have a man at the moment? Remember a few years ago when my parents separated?"

Annabelle nodded.

"You know what saved them from divorce? They started dating again. Maybe that's what's missing. You work, you have sex. You work, you have sex again. You attend events like this, but are you connecting in other ways?"

Her friend had a point, but how was she supposed to bring up the topic to Dante? They weren't supposed to be having sex in the first place, though he'd told her in no uncertain terms that they would. This wasn't supposed to be a real marriage, and in less than a year, they were going their separate ways.

"I'll think about what you said," she told Lacey.

The fashion show producer approached. "Lacey, we have some people who want to talk to you."

Lacey hesitated.

"Go. I'm fine," Annabelle said.

Her friend pulled her into another hug. "Thanks again for coming. We'll catch up later."

"Definitely."

Lacey rushed off, and Annabelle started toward Dante at the back of the auditorium.

24

"Careful," Annabelle said, as movers brought her lavender sofa into what used to be her father's office.

Clifton had officially resigned from the position of CEO, though he remained in an advisory role for the next six months while Annabelle became acclimated to her new position.

She had plenty of work to do and had meetings planned all next week to touch base with management and executives in the company. Additionally, she wanted to spruce up the office with new paint to brighten the interior from the dark walls her father preferred. All in due time.

Another one of the movers wheeled in her last bookcase. "Where would you like this, ma'am?"

"Over there." Annabelle pointed to a far wall. She'd need to add more furniture. Her father's office was much larger than hers, and her furniture seemed swamped in the extra space.

"Thank you, gentlemen," Annabelle said.

The men filed out.

"Hi, there." Julie, a member of the staff, poked her head in the door.

"Hi, Julie, come on in. How are your parents?"

Julie had frizzy, curly hair and an infectious smile. She walked in, looking as excited for Annabelle as if she had taken over the CEO position herself.

"Mother is deteriorating a bit."

"Oh no, I'm sorry to hear that."

Julie shrugged. "We expected her decline, so I've decided to extend the hours of in-home care. I need someone to help in the evenings, as well as when I'm at work."

"Makes sense," Annabelle said, nodding her understanding. "If you need time off to work out the details, let me know."

"I will, thank you. But the reason I stopped by was because I haven't had a chance to congratulate you on becoming our new CEO. We were all worried when we learned Mr. Buchanan was planning to merge with Strong Technology. I know you'll do a good job, and the company will remain intact."

"That's a priority for me. I'll be implementing a paperless policy and have a lot of other ideas. I have high expectations of you and the rest of the senior staff as we implement them."

"Whatever you need, we're behind you one hundred percent. Well, I won't keep you. I'm sure you have a lot of work to do. I look forward to the meeting next week."

She slipped out and quietly closed the door.

Annabelle walked over to the window. In the distance, Hilderbrandt Plaza towered above the other buildings in downtown Houston. Today she'd moved into her new office, and today Dante was having lunch with Nolson.

She should wish him good luck. Plucking her phone from her purse, she was about to tap out a text but stopped. They were in a good place right now, but was this too much?

Surely not. Dante didn't need good luck wishes, but sending him the message would be considerate because she knew how much he wanted the meeting to go well.

She hadn't requested date nights yet, as Lacey had suggested, but she and Dante continued to get along. They attended the usual social events together as a couple. A yacht party an oil tycoon invited them to. A birthday party for a close friend. Their calendar was also booked months in advance with events like dinner with executives and their wives and an auction at a private club to raise money for the homeless.

Nonetheless, theirs wasn't a normal marriage, despite sleeping in the same room each night and enjoying each other's body.

Annabelle put down the phone and sat behind the desk. She went to work on projections for the next quarter but couldn't concentrate.

There was nothing wrong with reaching out to Dante. Their relationship had progressed to the point that sending a text in the middle of the day shouldn't seem strange. He'd probably appreciate the encouraging words—she hoped.

She picked up the phone and quickly typed the message before she lost the nerve: *Best of luck at your lunch today! I have my fingers crossed for you.* Then she went back to work.

Several minutes passed before he responded. *Gracias. Cross your toes as well.*

She smiled and bit her bottom lip. She could hear the drawl of his lightly accented voice in the words.

I will, she typed back.

She placed the phone on the desk, the conversation with Lacey coming back to her again.

Tonight, for sure. She'd discuss a more conventional arrangement to their marriage and hope he didn't think she'd lost her mind.

৩৯৩

ANNABELLE AND DANTE ATE DINNER IN THE BACK OF THE house, overlooking the pool. Viviana had prepared *carne mechada*, Venezuelan shredded beef, one of Dante's favorite dishes. Packed with flavor from the onions, peppers, and cumin, he called it comfort food.

During the meal, he expressed his optimism after the conversation with Nolson. Nolson hadn't given him a final price yet, but he was closer to his goal of owning the iconic building.

When the meal ended, a member of the staff came out and cleared away the dishes.

"Will you be having dessert tonight?" she asked.

"Nothing for me," Dante said.

"Nothing for me, either. That's it for tonight," Annabelle said, dismissing her with a smile.

The young woman nodded and left them alone.

"What's on your mind?" Across the table, Dante watched her with a question in his eyes.

"What makes you think there's something on my mind?"

"I've come to know you very well in the past few months. There's definitely something on your mind, whether or not you tell me."

They'd become so close he could read her moods. She was able to do the same with him. She knew when he experienced problems at work because he entered the house with his brow puckered and a solemn expression on his face. If the day passed with few problems or he closed a lucrative deal, his step was lighter and his face more open.

"I was thinking about something. It's just an idea." Annabelle's stomach knotted tighter than a sailor's hitch. "What if we go out every now and again, as a couple?"

His eyes narrowed a fraction. "We already do. We have invitations to attend events all the way through the fall."

"No, I mean..." She hated asking for this. Making the request was almost humiliating, but she swallowed her pride and lifted her head higher. "I want you to take me out. Not like going to the fashion show or Nolson's party or the gala we went to last week. A date. Just the two of us, spending time together." She stopped and held her breath, refusing to lower her gaze though she desperately wanted to.

Dante extended his hand to her. "Come here."

She walked over to him but stood out of arm's reach.

"Come here, *querida*."

She edged close enough for him to take her hand and pull her between his legs. "If I take you on a date, will that stop you from becoming cranky?"

"I'm never cranky," Annabelle said haughtily.

He chuckled, his eyes lighting up and the dimples in his cheeks deepening. God, he was handsome when he laughed. His dark eyes lit up, the dimples appeared, and his entire face transformed into a softer expression. Longing coupled with fear burned in her chest. How would she survive when they ended their marriage?

Don't think about it.

"Will going on a date keep you agreeable?" Dante amended.

"Maybe."

His expression turned serious. "If you want to go on a date, I will take you on a date."

"Is that something you want to do too?" Annabelle asked. There was no point in going forward with these plans if Dante didn't want to do it.

"Very much." He pulled her onto his lap, and she wrapped her arms around his neck.

Face to face, they gazed into each other's eyes.

Cradling the back of her head, Dante kissed her, and she melted against him.

"Whatever *la reina* wants, she can have," he whispered.

Annabelle cupped his hard jaw and kissed him harder, feeling as if her soul was about to crack open. A torrent of emotions unleashed inside of her because what he said wasn't exactly true. She couldn't have whatever she wanted.

She wanted the one thing she doubted had ever belonged to her. The one thing she certainly couldn't have now.

His heart.

25

Dante helped Annabelle down from the SUV.

Without planning, they ended up matching for their date, and he considered the coincidence a good sign. He wore a white shirt and navy pants, while she wore a blue and white dress with an A-line skirt and puffy sleeves. Her hair was magnificent in a curly Afro with blonde highlights, sitting on her shoulders and framing her lovely face.

"I'll call you when we're ready to leave," he said to the driver.

"Yes, sir."

With his hand at her lower back, Dante guided Annabelle toward the entrance of the Museum of Fine Arts, one of twenty museums in the Houston Museum District and one of the largest art museums in the United States.

Since Annabelle was a collector and lover of art, he guessed she'd enjoy this first part of their night out together. The museum had scored a major coup with the acquisition of Satellite, a 24-foot-high bronze sculpture by Black artist and renowned sculptor Simone Leigh. When he told Annabelle they would be going to see the piece, she'd expressed excitement, as he'd expected.

The sculpture weighed three tons and consisted of a torso

with a disc-like head and paid homage to the undervalued physical and intellectual labor of Black women. They encountered the magnificent piece near the entrance to the building for modern and contemporary art.

Annabelle gasped as she gaped at it with the other visitors. "It's better than I expected," she breathed.

"I see why she's considered a star in the art world," Dante said.

They spent time appreciating the sculpture and then went inside the museum. Slowly, they walked the wide-open spaces, admiring the other sculptures and paintings hung on the walls. They spent a couple of hours reviewing the artists' works, whispering to each other as they analyzed various pieces. By the time they exited the building, they were both hungry and ready for dinner.

With more than 10,000 restaurants in the city, Houstonians loved to eat out, reportedly more than any other city in the U.S. As a result, cuisine choices ran the gamut from tamales to BBQ to Viet-Cajun crawfish.

Dante had chosen an old haunt in a not-so-nice part of town. The little known restaurant named Sabor was owned by married chefs—one from El Salvador and the other from the Philippines. They served a fusion of Central American and Southeast Asian flavors to create unique dishes.

"You want to eat *here?*" Annabelle asked, taking Dante's hand as she descended the SUV.

"Do you trust me?" he asked.

She shot another glance at the building. Peeling paint hinted at years of neglect, and graffiti marred the weathered bricks of the front facade. The neon sign flickered off and on and did a poor job of illuminating their surroundings, instead casting an eerie glow on the cracks in the parking lot asphalt.

"Have you eaten here before?" Annabelle asked, wrinkling her nose.

"Many times."

Her eyebrows raised in surprise.

After a moment, she nodded. "Yes, I trust you."

Dante led the way inside. The interior of the restaurant was in much better shape—cheery, in direct contrast to the forlorn exterior. There were white walls and clean, black and white tile on the floor. Pristine white tablecloths covered each table, and the scent of spices and other aromas perfumed the air.

Dante stopped at the stand in front, where a sign instructed them to wait to be seated.

"Well, well, well, look who's here." Ray, one of the waiters, greeted them with a big smile on his face. He was going prematurely gray, his hair pulled into a short ponytail.

Dante gripped his hand in a firm handshake. "If I knew you were working tonight, I would have come on another night."

Ray laughed. "Don't try to embarrass me in front of your guest. You know you love me." He extended a hand to Annabelle. "I'm Ray."

"Annabelle."

Dante placed a hand on her lower back. "This is my wife."

Ray's eyebrows shot higher. "I heard you got married. Congratulations. Annabelle, my deepest condolences."

She giggled. "I like him."

"Of course you do," Dante said dryly.

"Come on, let me take you to one of the best seats in the house."

Ray showed them to a table next to a wall of windows with a view of the parking lot.

After taking their drink orders, he asked Annabelle what she was in the mood for. "Or if you like, I can make a recommendation," he added.

She scanned the menu that he placed on the table. "I'd love a recommendation. Tell me about your seafood options."

Ray pointed to a dish. "All our meals are delicious, just ask Dante. But the salmon is one of our most popular dishes, and if you enjoy turnips, you'll absolutely love the turnip and mushroom sides that come with it. The whole fish is another popular menu item, elevated by the mint chutney it's served with. You can't go wrong with either."

Annabelle tapped her lush mouth, and Dante's eyes idled on her features, the way her brow creased as she focused. She always had a hard time deciding what to order.

Finally, she sighed and handed over her menu. "I'll take the salmon. I haven't had salmon in a while."

"And what about you?" Ray asked Dante.

"The whole fish."

Ray scribbled on his notepad. "Got it. Would you like an appetizer to start?"

"Nothing for me. I want to save room for dessert," Annabelle said.

"Dante...?" Ray lifted an inquiring eyebrow.

"What my wife said." He handed over his menu. "Who's in the kitchen tonight?"

"Dolly. I'll let her know you're here."

When they were alone again, Annabelle looked at him with curiosity in her eyes. "How do you know this restaurant and the people?"

"It's a long story, but I'll give you the short version. Dolly is from the Philippines, and her husband, Rafe, is from El Salvador. They take turns running the kitchen. Since she's working tonight, he'll work tomorrow, and she'll be off. They've been at this location for years, and every night right before closing, instead of throwing out the food they have left, they prepare plates and distribute them to anyone who comes to the back door."

"You were one of those people," Annabelle guessed.

Dante nodded. "One night, I asked Dolly if they needed help in the kitchen. I offered to literally work for food. To this day, I don't know if they really needed help, but several nights a week, I came in and cleaned, mopped the floors, washed dishes, whatever they asked me to do. In exchange, I received extra food."

Which meant he could send more money to his family in Venezuela.

"You had a rough start," Annabelle said, her voice low and compassion in her eyes.

"I did, but thanks to people like Rafe and Dolly, I did okay. They are good people but stubborn. I offered to move them to a new location, but they refused. They said they can help more people in this part of town. I offered to fix their building, but they said its condition is part of the charm."

He laughed to himself, shaking his head.

"Dante!" A petite Asian woman appeared beside the table with her hair in a ponytail and a long, stained apron tied around her waist.

Dante immediately came to his feet.

"I can't hug you, I'm filthy," she said.

"You know I don't care." He pulled her into his embrace.

She laughed and squeezed him back, her small hands lovingly patting his back.

He enjoyed coming to see Dolly and Rafe whenever possible. To them, he wasn't *el diablo guapo*. He was simply Dante, a rough-neck kid who'd done good.

"This must be your beautiful wife." She clasped Annabelle's hand in hers, and to his surprise, Annabelle stood and gave her a hug, too.

"Nice to meet you," Annabelle said.

"I am happy to finally meet you. He has spoken very highly of you, but I won't embarrass him." Dolly looked fondly at Dante while continuing to hold on to Annabelle's hand. "Do you know your husband is very hard-headed?"

"I thought you weren't going to embarrass me," Dante reminded her.

"Hard-headed? That comes as no surprise," Annabelle said.

Dante glowered at her, and both women laughed.

"Did he tell you that he wanted to move us to a new building?"

"Yes, he did."

"He's always trying to do something for us, and we keep telling him he does not owe us anything. So now he hires us to cater business meetings, and once a year at Christmas, he buys out the restaurant for an entire day, and everyone at the homeless shelter nearby eats for free." She patted Annabelle's hand. "Please take good care of him. He is a good man."

"I will," Annabelle said in a solemn tone, meeting Dante's eyes.

"I will leave you both to your meal. Dante, it is good to see you, as always. I'll tell Rafe you stopped by."

They sat down, and Annabelle stared at Dante from across the table.

"What do you want to ask?"

She carefully straightened her napkin across her lap. "I don't know how to say this without sounding selfish, I guess. But you never brought me here before, even when we were first married. Why?" Instead of waiting for a response, she answered for him. "Let me guess—because you didn't think I'd appreciate this kind of place."

"That's not why."

"No? We both know you had a low opinion of me." She sounded hurt.

"On the contrary, I didn't have a low opinion of *you*. Perhaps I had a low opinion of myself."

Her eyes softened and the corners of her mouth twitched. "You shouldn't have. I married you, didn't I?'

A smile curved his lips. "Yes, you did."

❧ 26 ❧

Ray returned with their drinks—an El Salvadorean horchata cocktail for Dante and a ginger and basil cocktail for Annabelle. She took a sip of her drink and her eyes widened.

"Oh my goodness, this is good."

"They don't make bad food or drinks here." He had tasted every item on the menu and never been disappointed with a single one.

"How is this place not better known?" She looked around.

A third of the tables were empty.

"By choice. Some people are satisfied with what they have. They don't feel compelled to work harder and strive for greater achievements. Dolly and Rafe are genuinely good people who exemplify this mindset. They are happy and comfortable in their current situation."

That's why he willingly supported them in any way he could. They had given back to the community for years without seeking anything in return.

Dante sipped his horchata and shifted gears. "Have you heard from Albert since the last time you saw him?"

Annabelle shook her head. "Not a peep. Are you ever going to tell me what you said to him?"

"I made sure he understood not to approach you again."

"Well, he hasn't. I half expected him to kick up a fuss when the board voted for me, but Daddy said they had a long talk over dinner one night—before he talked to the board. Albert was furious and tried to change his mind. He left the dinner early and told my father that he'd regret his decision. Daddy thought what he said might have been a threat, but he wasn't sure."

"The decision was your father and the board's to make, and he had no right to threaten you or your father."

"True. Hopefully, he won't cause problems in the industry. He could possibly try to tarnish our reputation or badmouth me and my performance now that I'm the head of the company. I never thanked you for... running interference. At the time, I was worried if you spoke to Albert it could sabotage my chances of getting the position of CEO."

"I know how to handle men like Albert. There was never any chance of you losing the position because of my conversation with him."

"Do you know what I wish sometimes?" Annabelle asked wistfully.

"What?"

"That my mother and Cliffy could see me and how much I've changed."

"They do see you."

"We say people who have died can see us because the idea makes us feel better, but I want to know for sure that they see me. My mother died before I had enough sense to figure out what I wanted to do with my life. She was always very patient with me. She didn't agree with my father's ideas about a woman's role. She believed a woman could do whatever a man could."

"Your father believes in a man taking care of his family. The idea is old-fashioned but understandable. He saw his father do that, and his father before him. The Buchanan men built a business and each male in the family was expected to take control when the time came."

"Are you old-fashioned too?" Annabelle asked.

Dante considered the question. "In some ways, yes, because of the machismo culture I grew up in. I have changed my point of view over the years, but I could never be a house husband. However, if my wife made more money than me, I could live with that."

"Could you?" Annabelle asked, her voice filled with doubt and one eyebrow arched.

Dante thought for a minute. "No, never mind."

She burst out laughing, and he was mesmerized by the sound. The rest of the world receded like an out-of-focus photo. With her bright blue-gray eyes and lush, smiling lips, he wondered what he'd do when they went their separate ways at the one-year mark. It would be hard as hell when their marriage ended. He didn't want their marriage to end.

"That's what I thought. You're almost as bad as my father."

"Almost, but not quite." He kept his eyes on her face. "His opinion hurts you."

She sighed. "Yes, but... he would never hurt me on purpose. I've accepted that he won't change. He's flawed, but I love him. He's my father."

They fell quiet, listening to the whispered conversations of the other diners around them.

Annabelle sipped her cocktail. "What made you approach me back then, when you and Sebastian crashed the private party at Lola?"

"I was desperate," Dante answered honestly.

That was the only explanation for why he had the nerve to approach someone clearly out of his league. The first time he saw Annabelle, his life changed. She was stunning, with the body of a goddess and a face meant to tempt mortal man.

"Desperate?"

He nodded. "Desperate to make you mine."

He knew he couldn't allow her to get away, guessing this woman would somehow change his life. Unfortunately, his obsession with her was quickly set aside for an obsession with success. He saw that clearly now in hindsight.

Pink filled her cheeks. "Why me? There were plenty of other women there."

"I only saw you."

The color in her cheeks deepened.

Ray returned with their entrees. "Annabelle, for you, the salmon, and for you, the whole fish." He placed each dish in front of them.

After ensuring they had no other needs, he left them to enjoy the food.

Annabelle peeped at Dante's dish. "Yours looks good."

Without saying a word, he swapped their plates.

She stared at him with her mouth hanging open. "Why did you take my meal and give me yours?"

"Because we both know you'll want my dinner, and I'll be stuck eating yours. I saved us both some time."

"I wasn't about to do that."

"You used to do it all the time."

"Ten years ago. I don't behave the same way."

"You weren't about to ask for a piece of my fish?" He dipped his head and looked at her with obvious skepticism.

Annabelle opened her mouth, but when he quirked an eyebrow at her, she quickly closed her lips.

Picking up her knife and fork, she grumbled under her breath.

"What did you say?" Dante asked.

"I *said*, you're a dick." She smiled tightly.

"I have a big dick?"

"No, I said—" She broke off when he started laughing and shook her head. "Funny." She rolled her eyes but was unable to hide her smile.

They both dug into their meals.

Annabelle groaned when she ate the fish. "Delicious, and the chutney is next level."

"The salmon is excellent too. Here." Dante extended his fork to her with pieces of salmon and vegetables.

She ate what he offered and moaned again. "Oh my goodness."

He chuckled.

"I wish I could cook like this."

"You could, if you wanted to," Dante said.

"Please, remember I'm the woman who burned the eggs the second weekend in our apartment as a married couple."

"You got better though."

She nodded and chewed. "Because I started spending time in the kitchen with Chef while you worked. I learned to make a few dishes."

One memory in particular came flooding back. "Then one night you cooked dinner, and I was late."

Looking across the table at him, sadness filled her eyes. "You didn't show up until after ten, and I'd made my first roasted chicken. I was so proud. But by the time you arrived..."

She shrugged, but he felt the extent of her disappointment.

"*That* was the final straw, wasn't it? That was the night you decided to leave me."

Annabelle set down her fork and knife. "I admit I needed attention. I didn't think you cared about me. I loved you, but I wanted more, and I couldn't figure out how to get more, so I went back to the life that I knew. And of course, my decision made you hate me."

Dante put down his silverware too. "I never hated you."

"If you don't now, you did. You weren't happy when I left."

"I was angry, true, but hate..." He shook his head. "I never hated you."

"Oh." She lowered her gaze and swallowed hard.

"For the record, I never knew your father's views on you taking control of the company. Or maybe I didn't see it because I was busy worrying about my own goals. Not only because I wanted to be successful and better than that boy from Caracas who came to America and shined shoes and washed dishes and worked construction. Yes, I wanted him gone." He paused as emotion churned in his chest. He had thought she understood, but she blindsided him when she left. "But I also wanted to be worthy of a woman like you."

The tug of war of emotions inside him was a nightmare. For so long, he had squashed his feelings for Annabelle whenever they saw each other around town and handled each encounter with ironclad control. For years, he had wanted to punish her *and* make love to her. He had wanted to rip her apart *and* hold her soft body against his.

Yet in a matter of months, she had run through his defenses and forced him to make a decision. He wanted her like he'd never wanted another woman, and the truth was, he'd never gotten over her. Annabelle Buchanan was his greatest weakness and the love of his life.

"You were never not worthy," Annabelle said in a soft voice.

Dante wished they didn't have the table between them. He wanted to touch her. He was helpless in the face of his need for her.

Immaturity had taken a wrecking ball to their first marriage, but he firmly believed they could rebuild with thicker walls on a sturdier foundation. They'd come far already.

They had put each other through hell, and for what? Pride. Selfishness.

They had both changed in a short period, and he believed only better days lay ahead.

※ 27 ※

Annabelle pushed open the master bedroom door with her elbow, carrying a tray with crackers, almond butter, and two types of jam. She loved to snack late at night, something Dante had found appalling. However, when she brought food to the bedroom, he indulged, despite his judgmental attitude.

Their first date night several weeks ago had changed the dynamics of their relationship even more. They were closer than ever. They hadn't established a dating routine yet, but they had gone out on one other date, this time flying to Vegas for dinner and a show. Dante took her to the casino he was going to invest in, and as they walked the property, he explained all the changes the contractors were going to make.

With their renewed closeness, it was like being in a real marriage, like during the first six months of their first marriage. She saw glimpses of the old Dante. The laughter, the sense of humor without the biting sarcasm or cynicism. The dirty jokes and double entendres that at times made her blush and other times made her horny as hell.

They were explosive together—not just two fiery tempers—

but two fiery desires. So hot for each other they damn near burned the bed when their bodies joined.

She participated in his weekly video calls to his family, and he joined her whenever she went to have dinner with her father. In between, they worked hard at their respective jobs and attended the usual social events together—galas, charity balls, nonprofit auctions, and parties.

Dante looked up from the book he was reading in bed—a nonfiction title about time optimization.

He groaned. "What is that?"

"Don't act like you don't want any." Annabelle climbed onto the bed and straddled him.

Sitting back on her haunches, she placed the small tray on his thighs. With a resigned sigh, Dante set aside his book.

"Tell me which one of these tastes better." Annabelle spread almond butter and mango jam on one cracker and almond butter and raspberry jam on the other.

She placed the one with mango jam in his mouth. He chewed, frowning.

"Well?" she prompted.

"Good."

"A man of many words," she said sarcastically.

He arched his eyebrow at her. "Do you want my opinion or not?"

"Of course I do, darling." She smiled sweetly at him.

She placed the other cracker in his mouth. He did the same, chewing while he frowned, deeply concentrating to give a good answer.

She waited patiently until he finished.

"The mango is better," he said.

"I agree. I'm going to have Viviana keep this one on the list."

She spread more almond butter on another cracker and spooned mango jam on top. As she lifted it from the plate, Dante stole the treat from her fingers and popped it in his mouth.

"Hey!"

He shrugged in a dismissive way.

"Greedy," Annabelle muttered.

She climbed off him.

"You interrupted my reading. That's the price you have to pay," Dante said.

"Whatever." Annabelle made another cracker snack for herself, but this time, she kept it out of Dante's reach. "Any word yet from Nolson?"

She tried not to question him too much about the deal because he was anxious to hear from Nolson about the sale of the plaza.

"Nothing yet."

"I'm sure we'll hear something soon."

"I hope so. I hope he isn't selling to someone else. Have you heard anything?"

"No, I haven't."

His head fell back against the cushioned headboard.

Annabelle placed the tray of snacks on the nightstand and straddled Dante again. "Is there anything I can do?"

He lifted his head and slowly exhaled. "You've already done your part. You got me a meeting with him, and now I have to close this thing. I don't understand what the delay is. He knows I'm interested."

"You're not the only one, I'm sure. And if he was talking to someone else before you..." She shrugged one shoulder.

"There aren't many people who can afford to buy the plaza."

"It'll happen." Annabelle leaned forward and kissed him softly. "What do you consider your greatest achievement?"

He smoothed his hands up her thighs, under the silk robe she wore. "The answer might surprise you."

"Try me."

"Being able to help others. As you know, I was a bit of a shit during my younger days."

"Only then?" Annabelle teased.

He smacked her right cheek.

"Ow," she said, though the blow didn't hurt.

"Helping others is what I consider my greatest achievement. My father was able to start a nonprofit helping other disabled people, Emilio has his app, and Marisol is in college for veterinary medicine. I also revitalized the old neighborhood where we used to live."

"I didn't know that," Annabelle said.

"We didn't exactly keep in touch after we divorced," Dante said pointedly.

She nodded her agreement.

"I'm doing whatever I can to help the economic situation in Venezuela by providing financial support, but the economists say we're a long way from a complete turnaround."

"Those are all wonderful things you've done, and I'm aware of your work in the Houston community." The local business media loved to splash stories about him across their pages. "I know how much you want this building and what it means to you, but if you don't have the opportunity to purchase—"

"I will." Dante cut her off with bite in his voice.

His adamance worried her. If Nolson didn't follow through...

"Okay," Annabelle said quietly.

The scowl evaporated from his face. "What about you? What is your greatest achievement?"

"I don't want to say after you gave such a perfect answer."

His face softened into a smile. "Tell me."

"Okay, well, it's not my greatest achievement, but my most memorable. Working with my father changed my life. After our divorce, I didn't know what to do with myself, and I went into the office to help my father at work after one of the portfolio managers resigned. Working with him and learning from him... I don't know. The experience opened my eyes to the possibilities. I'd never had to work before, and I liked it. I became confident and believed in myself, that I could do more than shopping and going to parties. I was proud of myself and decided to go to college, and when I finished, I started working full time at B&B."

For years, she let the general public believe she was a partying, empty-headed socialite, and at some point, she began to believe it too. It was better than revealing the truth—that she thought of herself as a pathetic substitute for the brother who had passed away.

"What about becoming CEO and saving the jobs of the people you care about? That's a very big achievement, no?"

"Yes, but I wouldn't have aspired to that goal or dared to dream so big if I didn't start small—in my father's office, helping him work—ten years ago."

"So leaving me was the right decision," Dante said quietly.

"No, that's not what I—"

He placed a finger over her mouth. "We both needed to grow up, and there's no point in dwelling in the past. We should focus on what's ahead. Our future business endeavors, and what happens nine months from now."

What happens nine months from now.

Those words smacked her in the face with reality.

Annabelle dipped her gaze to where his hands continued to hold her, his corded forearms dusted with hair and resting on her thighs. Sadness tore through her chest. She had hoped they had grown close enough to try to give their marriage a real shot, but he clearly didn't have the same point of view. He was thinking about divorce in nine months, and his words crushed her spirits.

She lifted her eyes to his and forced a lighthearted smile to her lips, though she was dying inside. "You're right. We had a lot of growing up to do, and we're better off now that we've had time to grow. I'm looking forward to what the future holds. For both of us."

They made love later that night, and she clung to him with

quiet desperation, determined not to give in to the melancholy which threatened to consume her.

She vowed to enjoy every moment they had together. In the end, if he wanted a divorce—she would let him go.

❧ 28 ❧

The aromas wafting through the kitchen smelled divine. Annabelle lifted the pan of roasted chicken from the oven and inhaled the fragrance of rosemary and thyme. Before Viviana had left for the night, she had given Annabelle instructions on what to do with the chicken and the accompanying sides.

She placed the bird on the stove and did a little dance at the perfect brown color. Tonight she had planned and cooked dinner for her Dante. He had never had a chance to taste one of her meals, and though they'd been married for a while now, she hadn't cooked because they had Viviana, his private chef, or they went out to eat.

She was a little nervous but excited for him to try the meal she prepared. It was simple but quite an accomplishment for someone who didn't normally spend time in the kitchen— roasted chicken, mashed potatoes, green beans, and candied carrots.

With a quick glance at her phone on the counter, she saw the time was a few minutes after seven. Dante was usually at home by now. She picked up the phone and dialed his number, but the call went to voicemail.

"Dante, where are you? It's after seven. If you're working late, call me. I have a surprise for you."

She had gotten the idea to recreate the dinner he had missed after they talked the other night.

Since he wasn't home yet, she hurried upstairs and changed into a red sheath dress and applied lipstick. Satisfied, she went back downstairs to the big dining room, which had been set with formal dinnerware and silverware. She had placed wine in a bucket, and there were two long candles on the table, which she lit to create a romantic atmosphere.

She had left her phone in the kitchen, so she checked it, but there were no missed calls or text messages during the short time she'd been upstairs.

Where the heck was he? He normally called if he was going to be late. Could something have happened to him? Knowing Dante, he had become engrossed in work and wasn't paying attention to the time. That had happened before, although he did call to let her know he was running late.

She busied herself with preparing the gravy for the chicken and moving the vegetables into serving dishes. By the time she finished, a full thirty minutes had passed since she left the first message. Okay, this was weird.

She called again. "Hey, darling, where are you? This is like déjà vu, to be honest. Want to know what my surprise is? I roasted a chicken, so you better get your butt home." She laughed a little, then paused. "Hey, call me, okay? I'm getting worried."

At eight o'clock, she blew out the candles and cut off a piece of chicken to munch on because she was hungry. At eight-fifteen, she poured the ice out of the bucket and replaced the wine in the wine fridge.

While she was scooping vegetables into glass containers, she heard one of the garage doors lift. A minute later, Dante walked in with his jacket thrown over his arm.

"Where the hell have you been?" Annabelle asked.

His gaze swept the food on the island in the middle of the kitchen. "At work. Then I went for a drive."

"And you couldn't call? I've called you twice."

Her fury dimmed when she noticed he was visibly upset. A frown marred his forehead, and the fact that he had gone for a drive was another clue something was wrong.

"What happened?"

"Nolson is selling the plaza to someone else."

"No."

His gaze switched away from her.

"Dante, I'm so sorry."

Her comment was met with stony silence as he stared at a spot on the far wall.

"Who is he doing the deal with?"

"Roman Dixton," he answered in a flat voice.

"Of Dixton Publishing?"

He nodded.

"What are you going to do?"

"What can I do? Nothing."

"It's not the end of the world," Annabelle said gently.

The look he shot her would have caused a lesser person to wither where they stood.

"You know how much I wanted this," he said.

"Yes, and I told you the other day not to get your hopes up. You know the risks. You've been in the real estate game for over a decade. Anything can happen."

"Do you think I don't know that?" Dante snapped. "Do you think saying I told you so is the best response right now?"

"I'm sorry, I didn't mean to sound as if I was saying I told you so, but sometimes, when we want something too much, it doesn't happen. I know how disappointment feels."

"You didn't want the CEO position too much, so you received it—is that what you're saying?"

His antagonistic tone took her aback. "You're twisting my words."

"And you don't seem to understand how important this was to me."

"No, I guess I don't because, as far as I'm concerned, it's just a building that you want for your portfolio."

"It's not just a building. The only reason we're married is because I want it!"

Silence filled the room after his outburst—the awkward moment that always followed when someone says the wrong thing in the heat of the moment.

Dante was immediately contrite. "Anna—"

"No, don't apologize. We both know it's true." She began putting away the food.

"Owning that building is very important to me."

Annabelle put away the last of the dishes and slammed the refrigerator door. "I know. It's more important than anything else. Than me, than us. You haven't changed a bit, have you? The real Dante was lying low, pretending to change so you could get what you wanted."

"You're wrong."

"I'm not wrong. I was wrong before, but what I'm saying now is not wrong."

"You're overreacting." His voice sounded harder and less patient.

Annabelle walked out of the kitchen before she picked up a utensil and hit him with it.

"Would you listen to me?"

She swung to face him in the middle of the hall. "What is there to listen to?"

"*Me*. I want you to listen to *me*." He hit his chest with a large fist.

Annabelle shook her head, heartbroken. Her love would never be enough for him. In his relentless pursuit of wealth, he had carved his path through the world with ambition as sharp as the edge of a sword. That was the most important thing to Dante Escarra, and he'd married her to acquire the ultimate symbol of success—in his eyes. Now it was all being snatched away, and she saw the misery in his face.

"I heard all the explanations before, remember? The truth is, you're an insensitive brute who only cares about one thing. Money. And you haven't changed. You're worse now. But kudos to you, Dante. All your hard work paid off over the years. You're richer now than my father and I are. The boy from Venezuela did good. You should be happy, but you're not." She spoke in a stiff, unnatural voice.

She continued walking away from him and went up the stairs to the master bedroom. At first, she didn't know what she was going to do, but then she realized she needed to get out of there. She changed into jeans and a blouse and Dante still hadn't come in. She grabbed her purse and headed out. Dante sat on the left staircase, and when he heard her, he looked over his shoulder.

His eyes zeroed in on her purse, and he came to his feet immediately. "Where are you going?"

"Out."

"Out where?"

She ignored him and descended the right staircase, heading toward the kitchen. But he caught her elbow and forced her to face him.

"*Where?*"

"To my father's!" she snapped, yanking away her arm.

"*Por supuesto*. The minute there is the slightest problem, you run to Daddy."

"This time you can't blame my leaving on your lack of money. The problem is *you*." Annabelle strode away.

"When are you coming back?" Dante called after her.

"When I'm good and damn ready."

She marched angrily through the kitchen to the garage and started her Mercedes coupe. As she was pulling out the driveway, Dante opened the front door. She couldn't see his face because he was backlit by the interior lights, but something about his body language caused a prickle of emotion to settle in the stomach. Guilt, perhaps for leaving? But she needed a break.

She hadn't expected to fall in love with him again and had been on the verge of exploding for a while now. Yes, she and Dante lived together in peace, but in the back of her mind, she could never forget this was all temporary. The knowledge that eventually they'd divorce and go their separate ways again hovered like a black cloud over her head and weighed on her more than she realized. She was a fool for trying to create a normal life for them. Date nights, regular sex, and now home-cooked meals.

She shook her head. His antics tonight reminded her that she wasn't very important to him, and this wasn't a normal marriage. They had agreed to a marriage of convenience, and she was a means to an end.

Blinking back tears, Annabelle waited for the gate at the end of the drive to open. Then she pressed hard on the accelerator to quickly put distance between her and Dante.

🦋 29 🦋

Annabelle sat with her feet curled under her bottom on the terrace of her father's home, listening to Katydids and the occasional sound of a distant vehicle's engine. She had helped herself to her father's spirits and fixed a glass of vodka and cranberry juice, which had done a wonderful job of calming her nerves.

The door behind her opened, and she glanced over her shoulder. "Hi, Daddy."

"Hey, honey. I just got in from dinner with Max and his wife, and Grace told me you were here. What's going on?" He kissed the top of her head and lowered onto the chair on the opposite side of the table.

Annabelle released a controlled exhale. "Dante and I had a fight, and I needed to leave the house."

"Oh. You fought, and then you left him at home?"

She thought she heard judgment in his tone. "Yes," she answered reluctantly.

Her father ran his fingers through his hair and didn't speak for a long time. Annabelle welcomed the silence because she was afraid of what he would say when he did speak.

"You shouldn't be here," Clifton finally said.

HANDSOME DEVIL

Her heart sank. "What do you mean?"

His chest expanded, and he blew out a puff of air. "Honey, when you fight with your husband, you shouldn't run off and come home. That's not the way to solve your problems. I regret letting you come home when the two of you were married the first time. I thought I was protecting you, but I... contributed to the end of your marriage. If you had stayed at home, you and Dante could have probably worked out your differences. Instead, I let you move back in when you asked, and... I don't know... Maybe I needed you here because I was lonely. Your mother had passed only months before. I wasn't thinking, and I was a little selfish."

Annabelle didn't know what to say. She remained silent, eyes trained on the reddish-pink hue of the liquor in her glass.

After a time, Clifton continued. "I also think I was too involved in your marriage from the beginning. Dante's ego must have been bruised when I supplied the apartment and the furniture."

"You were being helpful."

He nodded. "Yes, but my gifts were probably an insult to a proud man like him."

He was right. Annabelle saw that now, but she never saw the problem back then. Her eagerness to accept her father's gifts had probably bruised Dante's ego. When they argued the night he gave her the perfume bottle, he had confirmed his discomfort with her father's generosity, and accepting those items without discussing the decision with Dante had probably made the situation worse.

"If you want your marriage to work, you have to work through the rough periods."

"I know, but I don't know if it's going to work this time," Annabelle said in a thick voice. She twisted the Asscher diamond on her finger.

"Why not?" Clifton asked, alarm in his voice.

Annabelle shrugged, unable to tell him the truth. That their

183

marriage was never intended to last in the first place. She and Dante had lied to him and everyone else and pretended to be in love. Her father would be disappointed if he learned the truth about what she'd done.

"One thing I do know—running and hiding is not the answer. Do you love Dante?"

Tears crowded her eyes. Choked up, she nodded.

She had probably never stopped. That's why she'd struggled whenever she saw him around town over the years.

"Then you have to be willing to put in the work to save your marriage. Fighting is normal. I wish I could have one more fight with Priscilla. Her death was extremely hard to accept because of its suddenness. How could a headache lead to death? I would do anything to hold her one more time and kiss her one more time. If you love Dante, think about how you would feel if you can't see him anymore, hold him anymore, kiss him anymore. Think about what your life would be like without him."

There was no life without Dante. How could she possibly go back to life before their second marriage?

"You can stay the night, but then you need to go home. Your home is with your husband," Clifton said gently.

Annabelle knew he was right and nodded. "Yes, Daddy."

They talked for a bit longer, reminiscing about the days when they were a family of four. They laughed hard and shed a few tears before Clifton finally pushed up from the chair.

"Time for bed."

"It is late." Annabelle stood, stretched, and then followed him inside. She placed her glass in the sink and fell into step beside him as they walked the hallway. "Are you still enjoying being retired?"

"I've had my moments when I feel bored, but for the most part, I'm enjoying the time off."

"Hmm, I think I could find a spot for you at the company, part time, if you're interested," Annabelle said.

Clifton laughed and placed an arm around her shoulders. "Is that right?"

"I don't know if you know, but I'm the CEO now. I can make it happen. Submit your resume to my assistant, and I'll see what I can do."

They both chuckled as they climbed the stairs.

Halfway up, the doorbell rang, and Annabelle paused. Her father was a few steps below her.

"Are you expecting company?" she asked.

"Definitely not."

All the in-home staff had retired to bed, and the ones who lived off the property had left hours ago, so Clifton descended the staircase and went to the door. He peered out the beveled glass to the left and then cast a glance over his shoulder at Annabelle.

Her chest tightened. "Who is it?" she asked in a quiet voice, though she had already guessed.

Her father opened the door, and Dante stood outside in the same clothes he had on when he arrived at home hours before. The only difference was the determined expression on his face. He locked eyes with Annabelle.

"Good evening, Clifton," he said, continuing to hold her gaze. "I've come for my wife."

❦

THE CAR RIDE HOME WAS HELD IN COMPLETE SILENCE. DANTE was obviously angry, and Annabelle didn't want to say a word for fear of setting him off. She barely wanted to breathe. She sat close to the door, her fingers clenched together in her lap. She regretted leaving him at home, but there was nothing she could do about that now.

Dante pulled into the four-car garage and led the way into the house. He didn't say a word all the way up the stairs to their bedroom, where she finally couldn't stand the silent treatment anymore and spoke.

"I know you're angry with me, but I need to explain my side—"

He pointed a finger at her. "No. You do not talk now. I talk and you listen."

Annabelle fell silent and watched him pace the room.

"You are an entitled, spoiled brat."

"Wait a minute, that's not—"

He stopped. "You can talk after I'm finished," he said, voice hard and brooking no argument.

Fuming, Annabelle crossed her arms over her chest and clamped her lips shut but made sure to glare at him so he'd know how upset she was.

"I know I was late," Dante began, "and I should have called, but close to the end of the day, I found out that Nolson was moving forward with the sale, with someone else. Then I come home, and you attack me. I wanted to explain myself, but instead of being patient and understanding, you ran off to Daddy again instead of staying and working things out. And we should be working things out. At least that's what I think. I've done everything I can think of to show you how much I care about you, but it doesn't seem to be enough. I thought we were doing better, but maybe this marriage isn't what you want. The ring, the house, the dating, trips. Anything you want, I can give you, but you ran home again. Tell me, Anna. Do you want this life with me or not? Because maybe I've been a fool all along, and I'm not the man you want."

Annabelle opened her mouth to speak and then quickly closed it, waiting for him to say everything he needed to say.

"I'm finished," he said.

"I do want this—all of it, with you. I-I got upset. I didn't leave you, but I needed space. When you didn't come home and we fought, it seemed like we were making the same mistakes again. We were having the same problems, and maybe it's because... I'm not sure what *you* want, Dante."

"What do you mean you don't know what I want? I want you! I want us to be together. I don't want a divorce in eight months. I want our marriage to work because I love you!"

Annabelle drew in a sharp breath. "You... you do?"

"Isn't it obvious? How could you doubt that I love you?"

"Be—" Her voice cracked. "Because I didn't want to be the only one in love. The only one trying. I fixed dinner, and then you came in and said the only reason you're here was because of the plaza, and I—I was hurt. I love you, and I was scared our relationship was falling apart again..." Overwhelming emotion robbed her voice.

Dante's face softened, and he crossed the room to her. "*Ay Dios*, you drive me mad," he said, pulling her into his arms.

Annabelle gladly clung to him, burying her face in his chest and taking a lungful of air filled with the scent of him.

She gazed up into his face. "We were getting along so well, and then the night I brought up the two types of jam, you said something about us focusing on what we planned to do in nine months. I thought you wanted a divorce, like we'd originally planned."

Dante brushed hair away from her face with his fingertips. "That's not what I meant. I meant we have work to do, and by then, we'll know if we want to stay married or proceed with a divorce. Of course, I hope we'll stay married. That's what I want, more than anything. You and me, together."

"Me too. We can make our marriage work this time."

He kissed her forehead. "Yes, we can."

Annabelle squeezed him tighter, her thoughts on the impassioned words torn from his lips before she ran to her father's.

I want you to listen to me.

He told her what he needed, and she ignored him because she'd been busy thinking about herself.

"I'm sorry I left. I should have stayed and talked to you. We can do that now if you like," Annabelle whispered.

Dante rested his forehead against hers, and she rubbed her palms up and down his back.

"Yes, I would like that," he said.

🙮 30 🙮

Dante told her everything. He opened up to Annabelle in a way he never had before, and when he finished, she finally understood why purchasing the Hilderbrandt Plaza meant so much to him.

"I had no idea," she said from her position on the bed.

Hands in his pockets, Dante frowned at the tennis court. "I should be satisfied, but it's difficult to be satisfied when I've wanted this for so long and came close to accomplishing my goal."

"I wish there was something I could do." Annabelle felt helpless in the face of his disappointment.

"Nothing can be done. Soon, Dixton will own the plaza, and the possibility of me taking control of it will be lost for good."

The resignation in his voice broke her heart.

Dante turned away from the window. "Enough about the plaza. Dinner was delicious."

She smiled, perking up. "You ate the chicken and vegetables after I left?"

"Yes, after I became very hungry. Thank you for cooking me such a delicious meal. I saw the candles in the dining room. We should have enjoyed the meal together."

Annabelle shrugged. "It's been a rough night."

"Maybe I can make up for spoiling your plans for a romantic dinner. *Un momento.*" A devilish smile touched his lips, and Dante went into his dressing room. He returned with a rectangular-shaped box wrapped in purple ribbon tied in a bow on top.

"What is this?" Annabelle asked.

"Open the box and you will see." He placed the box in her hands.

"It's not a bomb, is it?" She shook it.

"If it was a bomb, I would not be standing this close," he said dryly.

"Good point, but you know I hate surprises."

"You love surprises," he countered.

She didn't deny the truth but couldn't think of any reason why he would have bought her a gift tonight. They weren't celebrating an anniversary, and there was no special occasion she was aware of.

Annabelle stood beside the bed and placed the box on the mattress to loosen the bow. She removed the lid and looked in confusion at the stack of papers inside. Definitely not what she had expected.

Dante wore an enigmatic expression.

"What is this?" she asked.

"Read them."

She reached inside and removed the papers. Scanning the contents, her mouth fell open when she realized what they were.

"These are share purchase agreements in my name for Strong Technology. I don't understand." She looked to Dante for an explanation.

"The shareholders were not pleased with Albert's performance at the company, which was why he desperately wanted to merge with your father's business and take over as CEO. Merging the two private companies meant he could exploit their synergies, which would have made the shareholders happy. Strong smart technology would have been installed in all the new homes B&B built and renovated. Unfortunately for him, he told the board the merger would take place, and when it didn't, they had another reason to be displeased. I acquired controlling interest in his company by negotiating with the shareholders and then entering into share purchase agreements with eight of the ten who wanted to sell. I purchased sixty percent of the shares and had them transferred to you. You now have a controlling interest in Strong Technology, Inc. to do with as you please. Albert Strong answers to you, in the same way he wanted *you* to answer to him."

Annabelle's eyes widened, and she shook her head in disbelief. "A hostile takeover doesn't happen in a day or two. This must have taken months."

"The day I went to see him, I made the decision to take over the company and give you controlling interest."

"But that would mean you started the process months ago—before we were married."

Dante's eyes became darker as he spoke with feeling. "We may have gotten married for the wrong reason, but I love you, Anna. I never stopped. When I say you're my queen, I mean it, and I want to give you everything your heart desires. That includes peace of mind. I never want you to have to worry about Albert Strong—not now or in the future."

He had essentially gifted her tens of millions of dollars. "I don't know what to say. Thank you," Annabelle whispered.

"That's enough for me."

She flung her arms around his neck and gave him a long, wet kiss.

Dante groaned and cupped her bottom. "I only wish I could be there to see the look on his face when you let him know you own a majority stake in his company."

"You can be. You should come with me," she said, cupping his jaw.

"No. Enjoy your moment and then tell me all about it."

☙❧

D<small>ANTE SWUNG THE CLUB AND LISTENED WITH SATISFACTION</small> to the *pop* sound, right before the ball hit the net in his office. The past two weeks he had concentrated on the deals he had working. He closed on business condos in Atlanta and reviewed photos, leases, and financials for two commercial properties in Mexico City. He put one under contract, which was scheduled to close at the end of next month.

Despite his successes, he couldn't stem his disappointment at missing out on the Hilderbrandt Plaza. Perhaps he had been *too* patient. He should have moved faster and insisted on a meeting with Nolson a year ago when he first heard rumors about the family's financial woes. At the very least, he could have been uppermost in Nolson's mind when the time came to sell.

Or maybe not. Nolson seemed to want to close the deal with someone he knew.

Dante clenched his jaw and swung hard again. *Pop*.

At least his relationship with Annabelle was back on track. They had such a full social calendar, weekly date nights weren't practical. Instead, they agreed to setting aside alone time for at least one full day out of each month. She was planning the next one and had insisted they agree to a staycation with no phones allowed.

The intercom chimed, and Dante walked to his desk and pressed the button.

"Your wife's here," Sebastian said.

He smiled to himself. He might never tire of hearing those words—*your wife*. "Send her in."

He set aside the club as Annabelle waltzed into his office.

"Hello," she sang, sashaying over to him.

Dante looped one arm around her waist and pulled her in for a quick kiss.

"When did you start needing to be announced?" he asked.

"You might have been busy, and I didn't want to barge in

like I did ages ago when I roped you into marrying me. See, I'm learning to be polite." She sat on the desk and crossed her legs.

"Finally," Dante muttered.

"I'm going to ignore that," she said dryly.

He chuckled. "To what do I owe the pleasure of your visit, *querida*?"

"I have good news." She smiled smugly.

"About what?" Dante asked.

"About the Hilderbrandt Plaza." Her blue-gray eyes sparkled with mischief.

"What happened?"

"I didn't want to say anything sooner, but yesterday, I learned from a very good source that the deal with Dixton Publishing fell through."

Dante's heart jump started. "Who told you? And don't you dare say a little birdie."

She let out a throaty, sexy laugh. Damn, he loved this woman. She was effortlessly sexy.

"While I was at work yesterday, Khuyen called to tell me the deal fell through, and she said Nolson has been an absolute bear to deal with—marching around the house in a foul mood because Dixton backed out."

"You're kidding."

"I'm not. So, guess what I told her?"

"What?"

The smug look again. "If Nolson wants to sell, you *might* be interested, but I wasn't sure because you had several deals working and the window might have closed. She begged me to find out if you still wanted to buy, which I didn't need to do because I know you do. She talked to Nolson about—as she put it—getting off his ass and making a deal with you before the opportunity slipped away. She called an hour ago and said he's definitely interested and would love to sell to you."

Dante clasped his fingers together. "Are you sure?"

"Positive. His people are going to call you this afternoon at three."

"You are..." He was speechless. Dante grabbed Annabelle's face and kissed her hard on the lips.

"Are you happy?" she asked with a wide grin, clearly already knowing the answer to her question.

"Ecstatic." He kissed her again, softer this time. He gazed into her eyes. "Thank you."

Her fingers curled around his wrists. "I want you to have that building, and I'm glad I can play a small part in helping you get it."

"I don't want to count my hens... What is it?"

"Chickens before they hatch," Annabelle corrected.

She burst out laughing, and so did he.

Dante shook his head. "Why do I always mess that up? I don't want to count my chickens before they hatch."

"I know you want to be careful, but I'm certain the sale will go through," Annabelle whispered.

Her optimistic outlook made him optimistic too. Finally, his dream was about to come true. "You're right, and at the closing, I'm going to make sure Nolson Hilderbrandt knows exactly who I am."

She smiled. "Dante Fucking Escarra."

❧ 31 ❧

D ante entered the Hilderbrandt Plaza with lengthy strides. The shoeshine stands were still there and able to accommodate three customers at a time. At the moment, there was only one man getting his shoes shined. Concerned with reading his phone, he didn't pay attention to the man shining his shoes. The old guy moved swiftly and with the dexterity of someone who'd done the repetitive task for years.

Dante took the elevator to the top floor, thinking about how he'd longed for this moment for more than thirteen years. He'd salivated for it. There were times he never thought he'd get here, and after last month, he was certain the opportunity was completely out of reach. But here he was, on his way to achieving the one goal he had chased for over a decade.

He exited the elevator on the top floor of Hilderbrandt Plaza and a pleasant looking older woman stepped forward with a welcoming smile. "Hello, Mr. Escarra. They're waiting for you in the conference room. Right this way."

She walked ahead of him to the end of the wide corridor. Soon this would all be his. The adrenaline rush of closing a deal was addictive, and excitement flowed through his veins in anticipation.

The windowed wall showed only one person in the conference room. When he entered, she rose from the chair at the head of the table.

"Mr. Escarra, nice to meet you. I'm Takia Jones, and I'll be overseeing the closing for the transfer of the property."

"Nice to meet you, Ms. Jones." Dante shook her hand, and they both sat down.

The older woman quietly left the room.

"Mr. Hilderbrandt is on his way. There's coffee over there, if you like," Takia said, pointing to a coffee pot and cups nearby.

"I'm fine, thank you."

"You're ready to wrap this up, I guess," she said with a knowing smile.

"Something like that." He smiled back.

"I understand. I never thought I'd see the day when the Hilderbrandt Plaza would be removed from the family. But I guess it's just time."

"I understand Nolson did not want to sell," Dante said.

"No, he didn't," she confirmed, with a rueful shake of her head. "The chemicals market has changed a lot and is very competitive. From what I understand, Mr. Hildebrandt's creditors have been less than understanding about his slow bill paying —allegedly."

"I'm sure it's been difficult for him. A man of his stature having to sell something of such importance and value not only to his family but the community at large. Perhaps the infusion of cash will soften the blow of his loss."

"Perhaps, although you negotiated quite a deal." The attorney glanced at the papers in front of her.

Because Annabelle had hinted he would move on if Nolson didn't move quickly, Dante had been able to turn the screws and secure a better price when they negotiated the sale.

"I was lucky," he said.

She arched an eyebrow. "Lucky? Everyone knows who you

are. You saw an opportunity and took advantage, and no one could blame you. You'd be a fool to pass up this property."

"And I am no fool," Dante said, relaxing into the chair.

Minutes later, Nolson strode into the room, head high. "Dante, I hope you didn't have to wait too long."

"Not at all. I only arrived a few minutes ago."

"Good, good." Nolson sat heavily in the chair, as if relieved to be off his feet. "Well, it took us long enough to get here, didn't it?"

"Yes, it did," Dante said evenly.

Nolson smiled at Tracy. "I'm ready to get started."

For the next hour, both men signed contracts in duplicate for the transfer of the building, and as he slid each piece of paper across the table, the drum of excitement beat louder in Dante's head. When the last sheet was signed, Takia stacked them together, and an assistant entered to make copies. After she returned, Takia placed the duplicates in folders and handed a folder to each man.

"Gentlemen, we are done. Mr. Escarra, congratulations on your new property. You are now the proud owner of the largest building in Texas and the twenty-eighth largest skyscraper in the United States."

Dante smiled. "Not bad for an immigrant from Venezuela."

Tracy laughed. "Not bad at all."

He shifted his attention to Nolson. "How do you feel, Mr. Hilderbrandt?"

A bittersweet smile touched his lips. "I wish I could be happy for you, but I fought tooth and nail so this day would never come. I don't know if you know the history of this plaza, but my grandfather built the original building, in this exact spot. My father had it torn down and replaced with this modern structure —bigger and better than before. The Hilderbrandt Plaza has been in my family for three generations and was a symbol of pride during all those years. I am truly devastated it will no longer be in our family."

"Good."

Nolson's startled gaze met his, and Tracy as well turned in his direction.

"Excuse me?" Nolson said.

"You heard me. Good. I am very happy that you're devastated, and now you will have to live with the knowledge that you are the reason your family legacy came to an end today."

Tracy shifted in her chair. "Mr. Escarra—"

Dante lifted a hand to cut off whatever she was about to say and kept his eyes on the man seated across from him. "I have waited thirteen years for this moment, and it is so much sweeter than I ever imagined it would be. You don't remember me, do you?"

"Remember you? What do you mean? I know who you are." Nolson looked genuinely confused.

"You know me as Dante Escarra of Escarra Commercial Real Estate, but before I became the man I am today, I shined shoes downstairs to make ends meet—among other things. One day, I asked you what it took to become as successful as you. I wanted advice. Encouragement. Neither of which I received. But your response stuck with me. I never forgot your laughter. I never forgot your condescension. And now, you will never forget mine."

Dante rose from the chair and took out his wallet. He removed the worn and wrinkled twenty-dollar bill he had carried with him for over a decade as a reminder to work hard, to persevere, no matter what obstacles dropped in his way. But also as a reminder to treat those less fortunate with respect and dignity.

"Do you remember this?" he asked.

Nolson's brow furrowed. "It's a twenty-dollar bill," he said, sounding bewildered.

"*Exactamente.* Let me refresh your memory. Thirteen years ago, I was a nineteen-year-old kid who had only been in this country for a couple of years. I didn't have the best clothes. I didn't speak English well. I never went to an Ivy League school.

Yet you did all those things, and here you are, struggling to keep your family's business afloat. Struggling—allegedly—to pay your bills. Your situation is so dire, you needed the money from the sale of this building, a building that has been in your family for decades. How does it feel, Nolson, to know you're the reason Hilderbrandt Plaza will no longer be a part of your family's legacy? Your fancy education, your expensive clothes—none of the things you claimed I needed were enough. You know what I think? I think that means they don't matter. I think you were just an asshole trying to make me feel like shit so you could feel better about yourself."

As he spoke, he knew the exact moment the memory came back to Nolson. The light of acknowledgment filled his eyes, and his mouth fell open.

Dante tossed the twenty-dollar bill across the table, and it landed in front of Nolson. "You can have it back. I no longer have a need for it."

Nolson's face turned beet red. The stillness in the room was so intense, the slightest movement would have shattered the silence.

Dante scraped up the folder with his paperwork and walked out of the conference room.

He made his way down the corridor to the elevator and took it to the first floor. He walked out the front door into the chilly air and turned left, toward the black Lincoln Navigator waiting at the corner. As he approached, the driver jumped out of the front and opened the back door. Dante slid onto the seat beside Annabelle.

"Did you get it?" she asked.

"Of course," Dante answered.

She squealed and leaned over, kissing his cheek. "Was he shocked?"

"He didn't remember me at first, but when he did, his mouth fell open."

A big smile broke on her face. "Congratulations."

He took her hand and pressed his lips to her knuckles. "Thank you, *querida—mi reina.*"

He couldn't have bought the building without her. Together, they were unstoppable.

"Where to, Mr. Escarra?" the driver asked as he started the vehicle.

"Home, then the airport."

By the time they arrived in River Oaks, the staff should have finished packing their luggage for the trip south. He and Annabelle were taking a few days off to spend Thanksgiving with his family in Venezuela.

His wife rested her head against his shoulder, and he threaded his fingers through hers. More than ever, he believed they were meant for each other. They had simply needed time apart to grow into the best versions of themselves and come back together to be a better, stronger couple than before.

BONUS CONTENT

If you enjoyed this story, join my mailing list to read a bonus scene with Dante and Annabelle in the future with their children!

Use the QR code or enter the link below in your browser.

geni.us/DDBonusContent

MORE QUICKSAND BOOKS BY DELANEY DIAMOND

A Powerful Attraction (Quicksand #1)

Alex Barraza was only supposed to have dinner with his employee, Sherry Westbrook, but their attraction cannot be denied. They decide to keep their affair a secret, but what happens when Sherry learns the truth about him?

Without You (Quicksand #2)

After years of cheating, Charisse finally walked away from Terrence "T-Murder" Burrell, but he wants her back. When trust is broken, can it ever be repaired?

Never Again (Quicksand #3)

Carlos Hortado receives a second chance to be with the woman he left three years ago. But he has a secret. When Carmen finds out, will she be the one to walk away this time?

Night and Day (Quicksand #4)

Anton doesn't know what to think of the sexy, baseball-bat-wielding firebrand who disturbed his weekend rest. But somehow he gets sucked into her charms, and after one night together, he can't get Tamika off his mind.

What She Deserves (Quicksand #5)

Layla Fleming has changed since her breakup with Rashad Greene, and a sex-only arrangement is all she'll consider now. But will that be enough for *him*?

The Friend Zone (Quicksand #6)

They have a great friendship, but a new man makes Omar risk their relationship to show Dana once and for all he's the only man she'll ever need.

Handsome Devil (Quicksand #7)

They might both get what they want in this marriage of convenience—
if they don't kill each other first.

MORE BOOKS WITH LATIN HEROES

Tomas and Talia are complete opposites, so why can't they stay away from each other? Observe their smoking hot chemistry in The Wrong Man.

Mechanic Ronnie is used to being in the friend zone with men, yet Diego makes her feel like a woman. Find out why they work in One of the Guys.

Check out the entire Latin Men series with heroes from Mexico, Ecuador, Brazil, and Argentina!

The Arrangement (Latin Men #1)

Leonardo da Silva is still seething from when his wife, Alexa, walked out on him. Now she's asking for a loan to help her brother, and he will help—if she resumes her role as his wife for two months.

Fight for Love (Latin Men #2)

Rafael Lopez, former professional wrestler and "Sexiest Athlete Alive," regrets the lapse in judgment that caused him to lose his wife. He shows up unannounced one day with some startling news and gets a surprise of his own.

Private Acts (Latin Men #3)

Samirah has met her match—in the form of a tall, hard-bodied sculptor who won't leave her alone. She's trying to keep a level head and stay out of trouble for once, but it's really, really hard to be good...when you're used to being bad.

The Ultimate Merger, a prequel (Latin Men #4)

Sabrina Porter leaves work intent on drowning her sorrows in wine and loud music at a local bar. Then she meets sexy Brazilian Renaldo da Silva, who's intent on showing her a different way to unwind.

Second Chances (Latin Men #5)

Renaldo's near-perfect life in Brazil comes to a halt when he finds out about his wife's betrayal, but he needs her help finalizing the biggest deal of his career. Will passion be enough to overcome the ultimate test of their love?

More Than a Mistress (Latin Men #6)

When Esteban makes an indecent proposal, Sonia's first instinct is to turn him down. But maybe it's time for her to use what she's got, to get what she wants.

Undeniable (Latin Men #7)

Abena wants to get married, have children, and live happily ever after. She even has a fiancé to achieve her goals. But two things stand in her way: Santiago Vila, and her undeniable attraction to him.

Audiobook samples and free short stories available at www.delaneydiamond.com.

ABOUT THE AUTHOR

Delaney Diamond is the USA Today Bestselling Author of sensual, passionate romance novels. Originally from the U.S. Virgin Islands, she now lives in Atlanta, Georgia. She reads romance novels, mysteries, thrillers, and a fair amount of nonfiction. When she's not busy reading or writing, she's in the kitchen trying out new recipes, dining at one of her favorite restaurants, or traveling to an interesting locale.

Enjoy free reads on her website. Join her mailing list to get sneak peeks, notices of sale prices, and find out about new releases.

Join her mailing list
www.delaneydiamond.com

facebook.com/DelaneyDiamond
instagram.com/delaneydiamondbooks
x.com/DelaneyDiamond
pinterest.com/delaneydiamond